Never-ending Acclaim for Fred Chappell's

I AM ONE OF YOU FOREVER

"I am honestly convinced that Fred Chappell is one of the finest writers of this time, one of the rare and precious few who are truly 'major.' I think that this is his finest work so far."
—GEORGE GARRETT

"There is, now and then, a book I want never to end. This is one of those books."
—MARIAN RAMSEY, *Rocky Mountain News*

"If comparison were necessary—and, of course, it is not—Chappell could be ranked as a blood brother of Mark Twain."
—BETSY FANCHER, *St. Petersburg Times*

"*I Am One of You Forever* gives us a view of the deep and shining life beneath the commonplace; the language flat-out sings and what we hear are the bright-dark, old things of our shared humanity speaking their new, unforgettable names."
—CHUCK SULLIVAN, *Charlotte Observer*

"It is an amazing piece of work."
—MIKE MAYO, *Roanoke Times & World News*

"A gifted spinner of fictions that often verge on the tall tale, Chappell broods teasingly here on the nature of fabulation itself."
—*Publishers Weekly*

"The action is beautifully paced and prop⸱⸱⸱⸱ and the novel's economy is but one of its vir⸱⸱⸱ ⸱n, not only of the narrator but of each c⸱⸱ realized. Here is language, especiall⸱ ⸱⸱ ⸱t its finest. . . . *I Am One of You Fo*⸱⸱⸱ ⸱ad for its rollicking humor, its poe⸱ ⸱ra-tion of the initiation theme, a⸱⸱ ⸱ation of place."
—*Sewanee*

I Am One of You Forever / A Novel by Fred Chappell

Louisiana State University Press

Baton Rouge and London

1985

In memory of
Guy Owen

Louisiana Paperback Edition, 1987

95 94 93 92 91 90   10 9 8 7

Parts of this book first appeared—often in radically
different form—in: *Chattahoochee Review, Chariton
Review, Columbia Literary Review, Long Pond Review,
Red Clay Reader, South Dakota Review, The Southerner,
TriQuarterly, Writers Forum, Xavier Review.*

Library of Congress Cataloging in Publication Data

Chappell, Fred, 1936–
   I am one of you forever.

  I. Title.
PS3553.H298I15   1985   813'.54   84-23335
ISBN 0-8071-1216-X (cloth)
ISBN 0-8071-1410-3 (paper)

Contents

I Am One of You
Forever

The Overspill

Then there was one brief time when we didn't live in the big brick house with my grandmother but in a neat two-storey green-shingled white house in the holler below. It was two storeys if you stood at the front door; on the other side it was three storeys, the ground floor a tall basement garage.

The house was surrounded by hills to the north and east and south. Directly above us lay the family farm and my grandmother's house. Two miles behind the south hill was the town of Tipton, where the Challenger Paper and Fiber Corporation smoked eternally, smudging the Carolina mountain landscape for miles. A small creek ran through our side yard, out of the eastern hills. The volume of the creek flow was controlled by Challenger; they had placed a reservoir up there, and the creek water was regulated by means of the spillway.

At this time my mother was visiting her brother in California. Uncle Luden was in trouble again, with a whole different woman this time. Maybe my mother could help; it was only 5,000 miles round trip by train.

So my father and I had to fumble along as best we could.

Despite the extra chores, I found it exciting. Our

friendship took a new and stronger turn, became something of a mild conspiracy. New sets of signals evolved between us. We met now on freshly neutral ground somewhere between my boyhood and his boyishness, and for me it was a heady rise in status. We were clumsy housekeepers, there were lots of minor mishaps, and the tagline we formulated soonest was: "Let's just not tell Mama about this one." I adored that thought.

He was always dreaming up new projects to please her and during her absence came up with one of masterful ambition.

Across the little creek, with its rows of tall willows, was a half-acre of fallow ground considered unusable because of marshiness and the impenetrable clot of blackberry vines in the south corner. My father now planned it as a garden, already planted before she returned.

We struggled heroically. I remember pleasantly the destruction of the vines and the cutting of the drainage ditch neat and straight into the field. The ground was so soft that we could slice down with our spades and bring up squares of dark blue mud and lay them along side by side. They gleamed like tile. Three long afternoons completed the ditch, and then my father brought out the big awkward shoulder scythe and whetted the blade until I could hear it sing on his thumb-ball when he tested it. And then he waded into the thicket of thorny vine and began slashing. For a long time nothing happened, but finally the vines began to fall back, rolling up in tangles like barbarous handwriting. With a pitchfork I worried these tangles into a heap. Best of all was the firing, the clear yellow flame and the sizzle and snap of the vine-ribs and thorns, and the thin black smoke rising above the new-green willows. The delicious smell of it.

After this we prepared the ground in the usual way and planted. Then we stood at the edge of our garden, admiring with a full tired pride the clean furrows and mounded rows of earth.

But this was only a part of the project. It was merely a vegetable garden, however arduously achieved, and we planted a garden every year. My father wanted something else, decorative, elegant in design, something guaranteed to please a lady.

The weather held good and we started next day, hauling two loads of scrap lumber from one of the barns. He measured and we sawed and planed. He hummed and whistled as he worked and I mostly stared at him when not scurrying to and fro, fetching and carrying. He wouldn't, of course, tell me what we were building.

On the second day it became clear. We were constructing a bridge. We were building a small but elaborate bridge across the little creek that divided the yard and the garden, a stream that even I could step over without lengthening my stride. It was ambitious: an arched bridge with handrails and a latticework arch on the garden side enclosing a little picket gate.

He must have been a handy carpenter. To me the completed bridge appeared marvelous. We had dug deep on both sides to sink the locust piers, and the arch above the stream, though not high, was unmistakably a rainbow. When I walked back and forth across the bridge I heard and felt a satisfactory drumming. The gate latch made a solid cluck and the gate arch, pinned together of old plaster lathe, made me feel that in crossing the bridge I was entering a different world, not simply going into the garden.

He had further plans for the latticework. "Right here," he said, "and over here, I'll plant tea roses to climb up the lattice. Then you'll see."

We whitewashed it three times. The raw lumber sparkled. We walked upstream to the road above the yard and looked at it, then walked downstream to the edge of the garden and looked at it. We saw nothing we weren't prideful about.

He went off in our old Pontiac and returned in a half hour. He parked in the driveway and got out. "Come here," he said. We sat in the grass on the shoulder of the culvert at the edge of the road. "I've been to the store," he said. He pulled a brown paper sack from his pocket. Inside I found ten thimble-shaped chocolate mints, my favorite. From another pocket he produced a rolled band of bright red silk.

"Thank you," I said. "What's that?"

"We want her to know it's a present, don't we? So we've got to tie a ribbon on it. We'll put it right there in the middle of the handrail." He spooled off two yards of ribbon and cut it with his pocket knife. "Have to make a big one so she can see it from up here in the road."

I chewed a mint and observed his thick horny fingers with the red silk.

It was not to be. Though I was convinced that my father could design and build whatever he wished—the Brooklyn Bridge, the Taj Mahal—he could not tie a bow in this broad ribbon. The silk crinkled and knotted and slipped loose; it simply would not behave. He growled in low tones like a bear trying to dislodge a groundhog from its hole. "I don't know what's the matter with this stuff," he said.

Over the low mumble of his words I heard a different rumble, a gurgle as of pebbles pouring into a broad still pool. "What's that?" I asked.

"What's what?"

"What's that noise?"

He stopped ruining the ribbon and sat still as the sound grew louder. Then his face darkened and veins stood out in his neck and forehead. His voice was quiet and level now. "Those bastards."

"Who?"

"Those Challenger Paper guys. They've opened the floodgates."

We scrambled up the shoulder into the road.

As the sound got louder it discomposed into many sounds: lappings, bubblings, rippings, undersucks, and splashovers. Almost as soon as we saw the gray-brown thrust of water emerge from beneath the overhanging plum tree, we felt the tremor as it slammed against the culvert, leaping up the shoulder and rolling back. On the yard side it shot out of the culvert as out of a hose. In a few seconds it had overflowed the low creek banks and streamed gray-green along the edge of the yard, furling white around the willow trunks. Debris—black sticks and leaves and grasses—spun on top of the water, and the gullet of the culvert rattled with rolling pebbles.

Our sparkling white bridge was soiled with mud and slimy grasses. The water driving into it reached a gray arm high into the air and slapped down. My father and I watched the hateful battering of our work, our hands in our pockets. He still held the red ribbon and it trickled out of his pocket down his trouser leg. The little bridge trembled and began to shake. There was one moment when it sat quite still, as if it had gathered resolve and was fighting back.

And then on the yard side it wrenched away from the log piers, and when that side headed downstream the other side tore away too, and we had a brief glimpse of the bridge parallel in the stream like a strange boat and saw the farthest advance of the flood framed in the quaint lattice arch. The bridge twirled about and the corners caught against both banks and it went over on its side, throwing up the naked underside of the planks like a barn door blown shut. Water piled up behind this damming and finally poured over and around it, eating at the borders of the garden and lawn.

My father kept saying over and over, "Bastards bastards bastards. It's against the law for them to do that."

Then he fell silent.

I don't know how long we stared downstream before we were aware that my mother had arrived. When we first saw her she had already got out of the taxi, which sat idling in the road. She looked odd to me, wearing a dress I had never seen, and a strange expression—half amused, half vexed—crossed her face. She looked at us as if she'd caught us doing something naughty.

My father turned to her and tried to speak. "Bastards" was the only word he got out. He choked and his face *and neck went dark again. He gestured toward the swamped bridge and the red ribbon fluttered in his fingers.*

She looked where he pointed and, as I watched, understanding came into her face, little by little. When she turned again to face us she looked as if she were in pain. A single tear glistened on her cheek, silver in the cheerful light of midafternoon.

My father dropped his hand and the ribbon fluttered and trailed in the mud.

The tear on my mother's cheek got larger and larger. It detached from her face and became a shiny globe, widening outward like an inflating balloon. At first the tear floated in air between them, but as it expanded it took my mother and father into itself. I saw them suspended, separate but beginning to drift slowly toward one another. Then my mother looked past my father's shoulder, looked through the bright skin of the tear, at me. The tear enlarged until at last it took me in too. It was warm and salt. As soon as I got used to the strange light inside the tear, I began to swim clumsily toward my parents.

One / **The Good Time**

The first time my father met Johnson Gibbs they fought like tomcats. My father was still feisty in 1940—he was thirty years old—and restless, maybe a little wild beneath the yoke of my mother's family. He truly had married not only my mother but my grandmother as well, and also the mule and the two elderly horses and the cows and chickens and the two perilous-looking barns and the whole rocky hundred acres of Carolina mountain farm.

The sheer amount of labor was enormous. The corn, for instance. Three huge fields stretched in the bottomland on both sides of Trivet Creek toward Ember Mountain. Even standing above in the hillside road, you couldn't see the ends of these fields.

Evidences of toil lay scattered about the barns: old hoes with handles broken off or split down the grain, with blades rounded off to cookie shapes. My father dislodged one from a corner to show me; the blade was no bigger than a jar lid. "Look at that," he said. "You don't think your grandma got her money's worth out of this hoe?" He flung it in disgust and it flew up clattering against the long tobacco tier-poles, scattering sparrows out of the barn eaves.

But the hoeing that was agonizing tedium for us

seemed none so hard for her. The three of us would begin hoeing rows at the same time. I was ten years old and was soon left behind. In ten minutes my grandmother would have pulled ahead of my father; in half an hour she would have lapped him, coming back the other way on a new row, and clucking like a guinea hen. "You boys better hurry along now. Don't know but it might rain soon."

My father would give her an unbelieving stare, lean on his hoe until she passed, and then dig savagely, swinging like a lone Saracen knight fighting off Christians.

But no matter how hard the three of us labored, the farm was too much; and so we came to meet Johnson Gibbs.

I can't say how the arrangement was made. Johnson was eighteen years old and had come from an orphanage to live with us on the farm. Perhaps it wasn't entirely legal. My father put it that Johnson had been as good as sold into bondage down in Egypt land and that if he were wise he'd head back to the orphanage and lock and double-bolt his door so my grandmother couldn't get at him.

He was a big handsome red-faced man with an easy temperament. He smiled easily and blushed—which made his red face look positively fiery—and he seemed to have an endless supply of chewing gum and a talent for cracking it loudly. I knew he liked me because he tousled my hair and gave me gum. The Beechnut was his way of disarming strangers. He was a young man who had been mistreated. We found out later that his parents were drunkards, that Johnson had been taken to the orphanage for his own protection.

My mother—who was no help at the farm, since she taught school all day—took to him immediately. She loved boys—that was probably a big reason she married my father. She loved most of all boys who were quiet and cheerful and well-mannered, as Johnson was. And he was good-looking besides. When my mother was introduced to him her hands went automatically to her hips, smoothing her skirt.

8

Johnson's eyes were of a light blue color, and when he met my father they became lighter, almost transparently blue. His smile tightened, a quick animal reaction. There would be conflict between them—that was inevitable—but the introduction went off affably enough, and took place on a Sunday.

They didn't fight until the next day. It was a law woven into the fabric of the universe that these two young men were going to have at it; and Monday was as good a day as the Lord ever made.

They began in the road in front of the barn, continued down into the mucky cow lot, and over the fence, tumbled down the hill into the cornfield, then rampaged through the field into Trivet Creek, and it ended there in the thigh-deep water. In my school playground we would have called it a fair fight, no gouging or biting and not much kicking, but a great deal of awkward punching and grunty wrestling. My grandmother called it hog-wallering.

The predictable result was that they became inseparable friends. There they sat in the creek, torn, bleeding, smeared with mud and cow manure, laughing in companionable lunacy. They laughed and splashed one another and then began washing themselves in the muddy creek water. They floundered up the slick bank and, both on all fours, shook water from themselves like puppies. My father barked like a little squeak-dog, and Johnson began to laugh anew.

My grandmother and I were staring transfixed from the upper road. "Lord a-mercy," she said. "Just look what them crazy boys done. Your daddy's worse than that other one. Don't he understand he's a grown man with a family? And him acting like a shirttail youngun without a lick."

She described truly, then and after. My father seemed no older than Johnson, not really much older than I was. We three males might have been the same age. The women in the family represented good sense and authority and our rebellion against the situation formed us into a tight high-spirited company. The time soon came when we could hardly look at one another without grinning.

"What were they fighting about?" I asked her.

"To see which was the silliest, and it was a draw. Would you just look what they done?"

Two sections of the cow lot fence were torn away, the ragweed and jewelweed on the hillside flattened. They had trampled a shaggy roadway through the corn, the knee-high stalks lying broken and shiny where they oozed juice.

"Got brains as big as June peas," she said.

They were coming back through the field now, still laughing. Their progress faltered when they got to the bottom of the hill and looked up into the roadway where she stood. It was easy to guess what they dreaded.

"I ought to take a tobacco stick to both of them."

They arrived and stood looking down at the gravel while she scolded. "Ain't there enough work around here, you want to go and make more for us?"

My father turned and surveyed the broken fence, the trampled corn. He sighed, then brightened. "We'll get it done now we got ole Johnson here," he said.

"I pray so," she said.

Her prayer was about half answered. Johnson was a willing and cheerful laborer, and as strong as he looked. But he was easily led astray, and my father was born to lead him there. Conspiracies bloomed between them like thistles along a fencerow. It soon became clear that they would do the work, all right, but that they would streamline it, discarding all my grandmother's intricate little prescriptions. No more hilling the corn with meticulous care. And if something needed repair, they would get the tools and repair it; no more propping gates and doors with fanciful arrangements of rocks and board ends. When milking time came they led the cows to the stalls and milked them, forgoing the traditional protocol of having Red and Daisy in first to milk, and then Little Jersey and Blossom.

They did the work and claimed it was done. She

claimed it was only half done; but now for the first time in her life, perhaps, she was overmatched. And when there was nothing to do they were by God not working. It vexed my grandmother's conscience to see someone sit down and take an easy smoke. The sight of someone not working for a moment or two caused great catalogs of useless tasks to fret her mind, and she would send the idler to oil doorlatches or soak milk strainers or to find a length of twine just so long.

"While you're setting there you could at least swat some of these flies," she said.

My father said, "Who swats flies in a barn?"

He now produced instruments of idleness and perdition. He persuaded my mother to procure a baseball and a couple of broken-down gloves from her high school and he and Johnson stood in the road playing catch. They were owlishly serious about their games of catch, zinging the ball hard and sharp.

But the work did get done. The weeds no longer stood as tall as the corn, the alfalfa was pitched into the barns before the summer showers came to rot it on the ground, the milk was set out in time for the Pet Dairy pickup, the tobacco was suckered, wormed, and topped in due season. All this in spite of that infernal baseball and the other deviltry.

We had a dozen or so pullets in those years, and we would come across thumb-sized eggs in the grass everywhere. My father found a use for them. In the big brick house was a room—she called it a "sun parlor"—which my grandmother forbade us to enter on pain of her most fearsome displeasure. Here she entertained her infrequent formal company, the preacher, or ladies from her Bible Circle. Here she kept hidden away—though of course my father found it early on—the huge box of deluxe chocolates that Uncle Luden had brought to her from foreign parts, from St. Louis or Memphis or Asheville.

My father sneaked Johnson and me into the sun parlor on tiptoe and showed us the candy. "How's this for fancy?" he asked. Each candy lay shining in colored foil wrappers, bright green, red, gold, purple, nested in the velveteen-lined box. Only a few pieces were missing.

"Fancy, I reckon. Looks good enough to eat," Johnson said.

"Looks can be deceiving," my father said. "We'll be doing Grandma a favor, I reckon, if we test this stuff." He handed each of us a piece and we unwrapped them and ate in awed silence. Mine was a maple cream, and I've never tasted anything so good since that delicious hour.

"Now give me back those wrappers," he said, and when we did he took three fragile pullet eggs from his pockets, wrapped them in the red and green foil, and replaced them in their little nests. "Does that look okay?"

"Can't tell the difference," Johnson said. "Not by a frog hair."

He looked at me. I nodded, round-eyed. Conspiracy loomed out of the air everywhere.

We didn't stop until we'd eaten a good two-thirds of the box over the weeks, carefully substituting the disguised pullet eggs.

Then one Sunday afternoon two of my grandmother's Bible Circle friends, two chattering bespectacled ladies, came to call and she took them into the sun parlor. We knew we were caught, and the three of us met in earnest conclave behind the corncrib. Johnson counseled that we move to Australia; he'd heard that there was a lot of dairy farming in Australia.

"Hell with farming forever," my father said.

"Go to Europe, then," Johnson said. "See what them French women look like, what you hear all the talk about."

"Don't you know there's a war in Europe?"

Johnson nodded solemnly. He was eighteen years old; he knew about the war in Europe. "What're we going to do then?"

"We'll stand and face the music. You ain't afraid of an old woman, are you?"

"Yes."

My father looked up into the top of a black oak tree. "Me too," he said. Then he brightened. "But say, wouldn't you like to be in that sun parlor now to see their faces?"

Johnson grinned. "Yes."

My father instructed me to peep around the crib toward the house and tell what was coming.

"Nothing," I said.

They rolled cigarettes and smoked and looked at one another, smiling thin smiles. It seemed they wanted to laugh aloud but had better not; it would be bad luck.

"What do you think?" my father asked.

"I think we're pure fools to still be in this county," Johnson said.

"I wonder what's happening."

I peered around the crib again and reported that my grandmother was indeed coming.

"Let me have a look," Johnson said. He stuck his head out and pulled it quickly back. "She's coming, all right."

"How's she look?" my father asked. "Does she look mad? I mean, does she look real real *real* mad?"

"She looks like she's carrying a shotgun," Johnson said.

"Well then, I'm satisfied she's a little upset."

"Which way?" Johnson asked.

My father closed his eyes, deliberating like a prime minister. "Due east, I'd say."

And with that they took off running like ponies before wildfire. They leaped across the brooklet at the bottom of the slope, vaulted over the barbwire fence on the other side, and tore through the hillside of ragweed at amazing speed.

When my grandmother reached the corncrib she was calm and smiling; she was carrying not a shotgun but one of my grandfather's black-varnished walking canes. "Where's them trifling boys at?" she asked.

"They went off somewhere," I said.

"Yes, I expect they did," she said. She looked down at me fondly. "You weren't any part of these trashy doings, were you, Jess?"

In the past weeks I had learned a lot. "Part of what doings?" I asked.

"I didn't think so," she said. She patted my head.

My grandmother foretold that they would return when they got good and hungry, and they did. They had to be hungry to eat the meals that came to their plates. My mother and grandmother and I ate very well indeed, never better. Fresh cornbread and tomatoes and fried okra and chicken and biscuits with sawmill gravy. But my father and Johnson ate eggs three times a day. They got fried eggs, scrambled eggs, boiled eggs, eggs any old how, for breakfast, dinner, and supper. When we worked in the back fields their paper bags held greasy egg sandwiches.

"Say, Johnson," asked my father, "do you ever have a strange craving these days to scratch dust and cluck?"

"I have stopped dreaming about the underwear girls in the Sears catalog," Johnson said. "When I lay down to sleep, it's all pork chops."

Finally one evening they did get pork chops, which was the signal my grandmother was making peace with them. Better than that, even, was that she gave us a brief account of the society news. "Ellen Louise and Mary ain't too certain about their storebought teeth," she said. "They're afraid to eat hard candy or chewy candy that will pull their plates loose. So they set there and squeezed all them pullet eggs in the candy box and they would break and smear their white gloves and the box got all runny. I saw what it was right from the first, but they just kept on. They must have busted I guess twenty of them eggs."

Johnson and my father looked hard at the tablecloth; their faces got redder and redder.

"Now I know you boys didn't eat all that candy at one go. Because some of them eggs had been there for a while. A lot of them eggs were spoiled."

"Spoiled?" My father sounded like there was a stone in his throat.

"Spoiled rotten," she said.

"Smell bad?" he asked.

"Awfullest smell there is."

At this, Johnson and my father burst from the table, overturning their chairs, and rushed outdoors. We heard them laughing out there under the walnut trees, laughter so explosive it sounded like light bulbs popping.

My grandmother sat where she was, but tears streaked down her cheeks.

My mother asked her if she was all right.

"I'm all right," she said, "but I wasn't going to laugh in front of them. If they seen me laughing, Lord only knows what they'd do next time." She reached and patted me on the head again. "Don't you never grow up to be like them two," she said.

"No ma'am," I said, promising myself that I was going to grow up to be exactly like them two.

Johnson roomed with me in the bedroom at the top of the stairs of the old brick house. It was exciting to have a roommate, someone to talk to in the dark when the wind moved the big oak branches across the windows and stars winked through the leaves one at a time. I slept in the iron bed against the south wall and he in the tall wooden bed on the other side of the dormer.

We lay staring into our separate darknesses and I asked Johnson to tell me a ghost story. What better hour for one?

"I ain't no hand at ghostally tales," he said. "Hunting, fishing, baseball: that's my line. I go for he-man stuff."

"Tell me a hunting story then. In the jungle."

And he obliged, but he wasn't much hand at jungle stories either. I was ten years old and knew for a fact that tigers didn't prey on kangaroos. He left out so many important details that I had to keep interrupting with questions.

"Wait a minute. How did the crocodile get up on the swinging bridge?"

"Why, he crawled up the bank. How else would he get up there?"

"Yes, but you had him pinned to a tree trunk with a

spear through his nose. How did he get loose from that?"

"He just shook his head like a big dog till he come loose. You going to let me tell this story?"

"Sure, go on. I was just wondering."

"All right, then. . . Where was I at?"

"On the swinging footbridge with a mean gorilla at one end and the crocodile coming at you from the other. How did you get out of that?"

"I jumped in the river."

"You jumped in a river full of rocks one thousand feet straight down? You'd've been mashed like a bug."

"Well, I would've been," he said, "but there was a flood come along and filled the river up. I didn't have to jump no more than two hundred feet, I guess it was."

"It was a mighty quick flood."

"It was a great big old flash flood and a lucky thing for me. I floated along on it as easy as you please till I come to a nice big dry rock ledge and grabbed on and started climbing out. Only trouble was, there was a great big old snake sunning hisself on the rock. Big old boa constrictor snake about twenty yards long, and he struck at me like a flash of lightning. . ."

I turned on my side and fell asleep in utter disgust.

If Johnson was rather frail with jungle stories in the dark, he made up for it with his baseball stories in the daylight. He used to be star pitcher for the orphanage team, he told me, and by his own account the most stupefying phe-nom on either side of the Mason-Dixon. "They marched to the plate whistling a tune and slunk back cussing a blue streak," he said. "They never got good wood on me and only bad wood when I wanted to give my fielders something to do. I had them looking every place but where the ball was. I had them hypnotized, hornswoggled, and hooligated. They prayed rain on when I was going to pitch and I prayed it off again."

I balked at Johnson's boa constrictors but swallowed his pitching stories like they'd been soaked in hot lard. "Show me one more time how you grip that pitch," I said.

16

"Which one?" he asked. "I got so many I can't keep track of half." He scrunched his fingertips together on the edge of a seam and laid the ball in the heel of his palm. "This one here is what I call my Drunkard's Fancy. There ain't no way to hit this pitch because there ain't no way to expect where it'll be. Just somewhere around the plate is all you can count on. I seen many a heavy hitter jerk his backbone in a knot trying to get at it."

He had a cornucopia of pitches, all right, and enough names for them to fill a telephone book. Besides the Drunkard's Fancy, there was the Submarine Surprise, the Blue Flash, the Blitzkrieg, the Snaky Shaker, King of the Hill, Shortstop's Delight, Hole-in-the-Bucket, the Step-Away-Lively, the Chin Music Special, the Simplified Bat Dodger and the Advanced Bat Dodger, Easy Roller, Sissie's Powderpuff, Slow Boat to China, the Rare-Back-&-Letter-Rip, and of course there was always and finally, Old Reliable. There were others too, but I got lost in the thicket of them.

I tried to grip some of these pitches the way he showed me, but my hand must have been too small. It was amazing the number of awkward ways Johnson could take hold of our old tobacco-stained, chipped horsehide.

"I don't see how you can hold it like that and get anything on it," I said.

"All in the wrist," he told me. "I got a wrist snap like a bear trap. And the arm. I got an arm half steel and half rubber. It's a great blessing because I can hurl these pitches for a hundred years and never do my arm the least bit of damage."

I was highly impressed by whatever he said about pitching, partly because I'd never heard anyone use the word *hurl* before. I'd never heard *hooligate* either; and haven't since. I was so impressed, in fact, that I carried these stories to my father, who appeared to consider them thoughtfully before approaching Johnson.

"Jess tells me you're a pretty fair country pitcher," he said.

Johnson didn't back off a smidgin. "I didn't tell him

the half of it," he said. "I didn't want to seem like I was bragging, but I can throw a baseball through a brick wall or around it or over it or under it."

"No, you wouldn't want to brag," my father said. "I hear bragging swells up your head and makes your eyes bug out."

"I heard that too," Johnson said. "I heard that bragging weakens a man down so much he don't even enjoy shoveling horseshit no more."

"You still look pretty stout to me," my father admitted. "And that's a good thing because I've heard of a baseball team needs a pitcher come Saturday afternoon. You know Virgil Campbell that keeps a grocery store down by the bridge? He's got together a pickup team and wants to play some Free Will Baptist team out of Caviness Cove. He thinks he's got a pretty steady team, all but a pitcher."

"I'm the man he's looking for," Johnson said. "If he looks any farther he won't find nothing but worse."

"Of course now, these are just old farm boys you might be ashamed to play against. They wouldn't be in your league, I can see that."

Johnson grinned, magnanimous as Roosevelt. "Do them good to watch me. They'll get a baseball education."

"All right then," my father said. "I'm going to tell Virgil. He's awful anxious to whip this church team. He can't abide the hardshell holy rollers of any species. It means right much to him to show them up."

"I'll be there to mow them down and rake them into windrows," Johnson said.

I was nervous as a flea from Wednesday until Saturday, wondering how Johnson would get along with the True Light Rainbow Baptist team. They had a substantial reputation in our part of the county, and I'd seen them play once, rough and tough, a fair bunch of flail-away hitters. Johnson didn't seem worried in the least; didn't mention the game or even pick up a baseball until it was time to ride out to the game. He tousled my hair. "What you fretting about, Jess?" he asked. "You're as jumpy as a frog in heat."

We drove out to Caviness Cove and stopped at a scrubby level patch of cow pasture, got through the longwinded preliminaries, and started the game.

I am not going to make an elaborate chronicle of this game, which certainly did not achieve epic stature. The Rainbows came to bat first, and we might have guessed that trouble was ours when Johnson's first pitch rolled off his fingertips and fell with a soft thud on the lip of the mound. He walked three batters before he got the ball anywhere near the plate. But it was better when it didn't get there because when it did the big raw Baptist boys whacked it to the long empty outfield. A hailstorm of baseballs out there. The Rainbows would smile and mumble in the on-deck circle as they watched Johnson wind up and *hurl*. I believe they were saying *Hallelujah Jesus how grateful we are for Thy bountiful gifts.*

Johnson's wind-up was a spectacle of some magnitude. It proceeded with grave deliberateness as he raised the baseball to eye-level, then lowered it with agonizing slowness to his belly button. Then he closed his eyes and made a frightening tortured grimace. Then he lifted his left leg shoulder high and rocked his torso back back back until the knuckles of his pitching hand nearly scraped the ground, and. Stopped. Stopped dead still with his left leg cocked like a dog aiming to pee on a cloud and with his righthand knuckles brushing the grass blades behind him: a hunk of nightmare statuary. . . . Then he came to the plate in a windmill melee. Arms, legs, head, shoulders, and torso flew apart in every direction. The body of Johnson Gibbs seemed to disintegrate like flung confetti. How would these scattered limbs ever come together again to compose a man?

This delivery flabbergasted me but confused the Rainbow batters not the slightest. They stood watching this human snow flurry with patient amusement and, when the baseball finally floated out of the uproar, swatted it into the blue reaches where the angels dwelt. *Blessed be the name of the Lord*, and so forth.

By the middle of the third inning, the score was 23–2, and not in our favor. My father conferred with Virgil

Campbell, that eccentric man, and they went over to the coach of the Rainbow team and stopped the game, conceding defeat. He told me later that he would have stopped it earlier if he'd been able.

"But I couldn't," he said. "The first time I saw Johnson go into his wind-up I started giggling. By the time he delivered the ball—I mean, by the time he dropped it on his toe—I was on my knees with laughing. I laughed so hard I couldn't stand up. The more he pitched the more I laughed. I could've quit laughing maybe if I didn't look at him, but it was irresistible. Finally I was rolling on the ground like I had a green apple bellyache and laughing so hard the tears came out of my eyes like water through a sieve. If I hadn't remembered to get away from that barb-wire fence I'd be all in crazy-quilt scraps."

He had a point and I had to admit it, no matter how profound my worship of Johnson. I was puzzled how to behave around Johnson during the next few days. Should I commiserate with him or avoid mentioning the game at all? I decided that Johnson would be so gloomy that I had better try to cheer him up. The man capable of pitching a game like that might be capable of any kind of self-destruction.

Johnson was as cheerful about the game as if he'd pitched a clean no-hitter. "Anybody might have a bad day," he said. "Some days the old arm just ain't there, that's all. There's days when even Lefty Grove and ole Dizzy Dean would get knocked around pretty good."

"You don't feel too bad about it then?"

"One bad day. That's the breaks."

"I guess you didn't have many days like that when you pitched for the orphanage team."

"What team? That orphanage is so broke they don't have diapers to go around for the babies. They surely ain't got no baseball team. I never saw no kind of a ball the whole time I was there."

"What about those games you pitched that built you such a big reputation?"

"Now I don't hold with lying," Johnson told me gravely. "It ruins a feller's character something awful. You tell lies and people will get to where they don't believe one word you say and then where'll you be? But—"

"What but?"

"But I was bound to pitch me a ball game. I've watched baseball and read about it till my head was full. So when I seen me a chance to pitch I jumped at it. You think they'd let me pitch if I told them I ain't never pitched a game but I sure would like to try it one time? Thing to do was let on I was the hottest thing since Walter Johnson. Then they'd pay me some mind."

"Well, now that you've pitched, what do you think about it?"

"I think I better practice some," he said. "Maybe work me up a whole new assortment of pitches. I don't let it get me down."

"That's nice," I said.

He rumpled my hair. "One single man can't be the best at everything. Now what I'm really good at is trout fishing. With a fly rod. I can pull trout out of the sand and the dry rocks. You never seen anything like it. Them fish come flocking to me like I was their mama."

The bright happy days darted past us like minnows. We had the farm in pretty fair running order now. The weather held good and the corn and alfalfa were tender and green. We had already reset tobacco twice. Mucked out the milking barn. Cleaned the fencerows and mended the wire. And now when I remember it, it seems we were laughing and joking from one hour to the next.

We pleased our womenfolk, and teased and exacerbated them too. "Got to keep them on their toes," my father said. "Otherwise they'll go out and rent another farm just to keep us busy."

We had running jokes, pranks, passwords, and private signals. It got to the point that my father could look at Johnson with a certain facial expression and Johnson would turn scarlet and giggle. There was a way Johnson could wiggle his shoulders that I found intolerably funny.

A stranger observing us from cooler vantage would have certified us for the county asylum.

Johnson had a secret to tell me, though, which was no joke. He swore me solemnly to absolute silence. "When your folks hear about this they're going to have a tizzy fit," he said. "And that'll be soon enough. So let's don't worry them no more than we have to. But I'll bust in half, trying to keep it plumb to myself."

"What is it then?"

"I've enlisted," he said gravely. "I went down to the post office and joined up."

"Joined up what?"

"I've joined the army," he said. "Don't you tell nobody, Jess, not a soul."

"Don't worry," I said. "I won't tell, never." But I didn't understand the reason for secrecy. I knew that Johnson had joined the army so he could go to Europe and whip Hitler's sorry ass. What was wrong with that? My father was continually saying that somebody had to do it, and so Johnson, taking him at his word, had signed up for the job. It was a straightforward proposition. I only hoped Johnson wasn't thinking of taking on Hitler in a baseball game.

But then the army would train him to throw a better curve; the army was famous for training men.

"All right," Johnson said. "Now you know. Just as long as you don't tell."

"I done said I wouldn't and I won't." I kept my word.

For his birthday Johnson received a fly rod from my parents. He also got a shiny new reel and a box of dry flies. It was a first-rate rig and as soon as I laid eyes on it I was discontent with my old cane pole which had served me perfectly well for the past two years.

Johnson gazed at it with watery eyes. "It's a Shakespeare," he said in a choked voice. He laid it across a chair and walked out of the living room into the hall, going in private to wipe his tears away. He came back in and said, "I never seen one before, except the pictures in magazines. I never thought—" Then he left the room again, his face redder than I'd ever seen it before.

My father and mother stood by the wood heater, hugging one another. When Johnson returned once more, my father said, "That's all right."

Johnson said, "No it ain't either. You don't know—"

"That's all right," he said. "Nothing to say. Best thing you can do is, you boys get yourselves together and I'll drop you off up West Fork Pigeon and you bring us back a good mess of trout. That'll do it. That'll do it fine."

"I'm ready to go," I said, and Johnson said he would be ready in a minute.

The stream where he let us off wasn't much wider than a kitchen table, but it rushed by fast and we knew there'd be pools and broad quiet stretches above. We struck out upstream, dodging through laurel thickets and clambering over rock faces. We came to a pool all dark and silent except at the head, where the cold breathing water boiled beneath an eight-foot waterfall.

"This one just might do," Johnson said. "Let me try it a little bit with the fly and then you can bait fish it with the cane pole. Fly fishers have to go first, you know. All right?" He began to tie a fly to the long leader.

"What kind are you going to use?" I asked.

"Female Adams," he said. He showed me a bit of gray and brown fluff with a fuzzy gray collar which I didn't find impressive. "Sure fire," he said.

He began casting, standing ankle deep at the outlet of the pool. First he hung the fly in some low hanging sweet gum branches behind his left shoulder, then he hung it on a big lichenous rock in the middle of the stream. He grinned over his shoulder at me. "Buck fever," he said.

I settled on the bank to wait my turn.

He got the fly caught in the sleeve of his blue cotton shirt and while he was working it free the line wrapped around the rod tip. Then the fly hooked into his shirt collar. Now he couldn't see it so he took off his shirt, setting the butt of the rod on a stone. When the hook came out of the cloth the rod nearly flipped into the stream and he grabbed at it with both hands. His shirt dropped in and floated down toward me. I lifted it out dripping with my cane pole.

"Just spread it out on that bush," he said. "It'll dry in a jiffy."

"Looks like it might take you some time to get used to the new rig," I said and might have said more if I'd trusted his temper.

His expression was distant, his eyes glazed with obsession. "I don't believe this pool is just right for a fly rod."

How'd you know? You ain't got a hook in it yet. But I didn't speak aloud.

"I'll move on upstream and give this one to you. Ought to be a good baiting pool. Come on when you finish and catch up with me."

"Okay."

While he skirted a patch of sawbriar to head east, I bit a couple of lead shot onto my line and slipped a greasy white grub headfirst over the hook, careful not to squash his innards out. When I thought the pool had quieted sufficiently I tossed the hook into an oily ripple in the middle of the stream. In just a moment I got a strike as solid as a blow on the shoulder. I took my time and pulled out a black-filigreed brook trout about nine inches long. I disengaged the hook and knocked his head on a rock. I broke off a forky twig, slipped it through his mouth and gill, and stuck the twig deep into the bank so he could dangle in the water and keep fresh.

The sunlight then was edging over the treetops, and after I'd caught three more nice fish, it was level with my left shoulder, full and warm. I decided to clean what I had, and started after Johnson to borrow his pocket knife. I strung the fish on a willow withy, twisted it round my belt, and set off.

I found Johnson half a mile upstream. He was lying on a big rock in the sunlight with just his underwear drawers on. His tan cotton pants were spread out beside him;

they were soaking. He was lying so still he might have been dead.

"What happened to you?"

He sat up with a jerk. "I hooked a fish!" he shouted. Then he relaxed and spoke in a quieter tone. "I swear to God, Jess, he was as big as my leg. Swear to God. But I was standing in an unsteady place and I fell off in the water."

"Did he get away?"

He nodded solemnly. "I'll get him. We'll come back again and I'll catch him next time for sure." He lay back again and closed his eyes.

"Where's your rod?"

"Right over yonder. Ain't it a dandy? Come over here and set a minute, I'll tell you something."

I went and sat. "What?" I said.

He opened his eyes and talked in confidential tones to the blue sky above. "I ain't never been fishing before. This is the first time. But I've thought a lot about it."

"You mean you ain't never been fly fishing."

"I never been fishing period. Where's a orphan boy going to go fishing?"

"I never thought."

"This is the best thing that ever happened. This is the best time I ever had."

I listened to the rush and gurgle of the stream; there were a thousand voices in it.

"There ain't nothing better than this," Johnson said. "From here on out it's all downhill." He sat up and hugged his knees. "I bet the best time is over for me after this."

We fell silent to hear the water and the woods. Downstream below us two tall poplars stood on either side. The space between their branches was like a big window and while Johnson and I watched, a bird cut straight and quick through the space, gliding from one shadow to the other. But I couldn't say what kind of bird, dark against the light.

Two / *The Posse*

Word of Uncle Luden's visit came in the form of a post-card from Reno, Nevada, with his loose purple scrawl: *Make plenty that good cornbread, Il'e be there soon.* He signed both names, *Luden Sorrells.*

My grandmother didn't allow me to examine the post-card because it was a photograph of dancing girls naughtily clad. Johnson Gibbs sneaked it out for me and we looked at it for a long time behind the corncrib, but I was disappointed. A long line of girls taken from a distance and all the important details blurred. "I can't see anything," I complained.

He grinned. "You sure you know what to look for?"

Though the photograph was disappointing, the message was glorious news.

My father nudged Johnson's elbow. "We're going to eat fine now. Uncle Luden is the prodigal son. Any fatted calf in the neighborhood, his days are numbered."

"Prodigal son how?" Johnson asked.

"Just like in the Bible," my father said. "Uncle Luden will lie down with the swine. Or anything else handy."

The farm work that had got the best of us until Johnson showed up to help had disgusted Uncle Luden early in his career. My mother's brother had little of her sunny but long-suffering patience. In the back alfalfa fields he had found a dilapidated old hay wagon and had worked it over until it looked sturdy and bright and something like new. On his sixteenth birthday he sold the wagon to a gullible neighbor, bought a secondhand motorcycle, and sped off to California in a cloud of gravel and a hail of loose bolts.

In the golden land of opportunity he hauled down a job that paid actual cash money, greenback dollars that were as scarce as kangaroos to us on our scratchankle mountain farm. Now and again he would send my grand-mother a check representing some of these fabled en-tities, and he sent other presents too. I once got a nifty cap pistol, for instance, and my grandmother had re-ceived that box of fancy candies which had been the oc-casion of what she called "a lavish of tomfool."

"He seems like a right good feller," Johnson said.

"He was born a generous man and I reckon he's set to stay one, unless he took a notion to sober up," my father said, and added: "But that's not likely."

"Say he's a drinking man?"

"Yes, but not the kind you'll generally see. In fact, Uncle Luden is a different sort altogether. I want you to see how he does, Johnson, sniffing the breeze and chew-ing his ole mustache and patrolling the female gender."

"Kind of a ladies' man too, is he?"

"Oh, my word."

"I'm all wound up to meet him," Johnson said. "Looks like he'll be here in a day or two."

"He'll be here when you see him," my father said. "I wouldn't set my calendar by him."

"Is he bringing his pistol?" I asked.

"I expect he'll bring whatever mischief he can pack on a motorcycle."

"Carries a pistol, does he?" Johnson asked. "I hope he ain't no kind of desperado."

"Now you got it," my father said. "When Uncle Luden

walks the street, strong men tremble and women squeal. If you're feeling faint of heart, you'd better hide out in the woods till he gets gone."

"No sirreebob. I got to see this gentleman. I'd rather see him than Santy Claus."

A week passed before he arrived, and not on a motorcycle, but in a tall red panel truck. He had outfitted it to live in on the way from Los Angeles, and though his dark little quarters held a variety of interesting odors and other surprises, I was let down he hadn't roared in on the motorcycle. I wanted to learn that machine so that when it was my turn to escape to California, I'd have no difficulty. Just crank her up and boil away into the sunset.

He showed up right at suppertime and parked in the road below the yard. My father jumped up and cut the dining room lights and we waited in the dark. There was a mysterious Christmas feeling in the air, although it was late spring and the twilight throbbed with frog-song.

"Johnson, I want you to look at this," my father said.

The driver's side was away from us, but we heard the door open and—after what seemed a long time—close. We were so quiet we could hear each other breathe and the ticking of the clock in the sitting room. No one chewed his mouthful of food. Finally Uncle Luden's head appeared above the hood of the truck. He was a short man and all we could see was his head, moving forward slowly as if transported on a platter. He wandered to the front end of the truck and stood there to examine it. He took a big blue bandanna from his hip pocket and polished the hood ornament; blew his breath on it; gave it a last loving rub; folded the bandanna into a careful square and restored it to his pocket. Then he turned round to face the fields and the sky.

"Now watch him, Johnson," my father said. "He's going to smell if there's any whiskey in Osgood County."

Uncle Luden raised his face and breathed deeply; then began taking short whiffs of breath like a railroad engine

building up steam; and then took one final lung-
stretcher. He turned to face the west, the north, the east.

"Now what's that remind you of?" my father asked.

"Seems to me he's about one-half groundhog," Johnson
said.

My grandmother clucked her tongue but said nothing.

"Part groundhog, part mule. You ever see a mule eating briars? Watch this."

Uncle Luden began chewing his mustache. First he
nibbled at the patch beneath his nose but it obviously
wasn't altogether satisfying and he dragged the left side
of his lip down and his lower teeth went along the gray-
black bristles like pinking shears. Then again on the
right side. Back again on both sides. The unruly ends of
the mustache were left over and he tucked them into the
corners of his mouth with his thumbs and gnawed them
and sucked like he'd got a joint of sugarcane.

Anyone unknowingly observed seems to behave oddly
and even ridiculously. I would not like to realize that
somebody was watching me most hours of the day. But
with Uncle Luden the strangeness was much more pro-
nounced; I did feel that I was watching someone as different from me as a muskrat because I had the same trouble
in imputing motives to his little habits as I would for a
member of another species. He really was, as my father
said, a different sort of animal. Why was he now meticu-
lously inspecting his panel truck front to back, kicking
the tires and thumping the metal with his knuckles?

"He's brought that truck three thousand miles," my
father said, "and he's not convinced it's the same one he
started out with."

"All right, boys," my grandmother said, "you've had
your fun on Uncle Luden. Jess, run down now and welcome him home."

I was out the door like a sprinter off his chock and
down through the yard. Suddenly the trees had shadows and my own shadow was fleet before me. They had
snapped on the lights in the house. My uncle raised his

face to the glow, his expression startled—like that of a groundhog disturbed in his grooming—but breaking into a grin.

My father had prophesied that we would eat well while Uncle Luden was home to visit, and so we did. We got not only an unusual hearty tonnage, but saw for the first time since Easter my grandmother's chow-chow and precious pickled peaches, and she even made a lopsided tar-colored chocolate cake.

"I believe this Prodigal Son business must be a handsome racket," my father said. "We ought to try it sometime, you and me."

"I wouldn't complain," Johnson said. "Start off with a motorcycle and work up to a panel truck. Next time he'll be pulling up in a Cadillac."

Our lives changed in other ways too. The telephone which ordinarily wouldn't ring three times in a month became demonically possessed and began trilling every hour of the day and night. It was always for Uncle Luden, and it was always women women women calling, their voices audible with excitement all the way across the room.

"Oh, brother, you've got a telephone call," my mother would say, and Uncle Luden would look at each of us expectantly, then give us a communal wink and a happy smile, rise slowly from his chair and amble to the instrument. "Well, howdy now, honey," he would say. "Where's the party going on?" Those were his words if it had been Winston Churchill on the line.

"How do they know he's here?" Johnson asked. "He ain't hardly but just arrived."

"Instinct," my father said. "I've always thought that Uncle Luden gives off some sort of musk-odor that menfolks can't smell."

"Well, where are all these women at, anyhow? When I try to work up a date I can't find but a mighty few girls in the county."

"These are not your type, Johnson. You're not ready for this brand of female yet."

"That's where you're wrong," Johnson said. "You ain't got the power to fancy how ready I am."

One time I was alone in the house when the telephone rang. Uncle Luden was with the rest of the family inspecting a big hornet's nest in a locust tree and I'd dropped back to sneak a chicken leg out of the icebox.

It was a woman's voice in the receiver, of course, lush and giggly. "I'd like to speak to that bad boy Luden Sorrells right this minute," she said.

"He ain't here," I said.

"Where's he at?"

"He's out looking at a hornet's nest," I said.

She paused, then said, "You tell him that I happen to be sitting on a hornet's nest and he better call up Spanky-Sue the first minute he gets back."

"Spanky-Sue?"

"You tell him it's that little old Spanky-Sue and he'll know what you mean."

When they returned I delivered the baffling message that there was this little old Spanky-Sue sitting on a hornet's nest waiting for his phone call.

"Mm hmm," he said, and chewed the mustache ragged. "Spanky-Sue," he said finally. "Can't recall that one. . . Sister, do you happen to recollect who Spanky-Sue might be?"

"I just feel certain, Luden, that I don't know," she said.

"Mm hmm." He pondered for a time and then appealed to my father. "How about it, Joe Robert? Who is this here Spanky-Sue?"

"If I knew I wouldn't take this opportunity to say so," my father said.

"Mm hmm. . ." He gave me a slow wink. "Jess?"

"I don't know," I said. "Why is she sitting on a hornet's nest?"

"We all got our burden to bear," he said. "I wish I could think who she is."

31

"Maybe you'd better call her up anyhow," my father said. "She might be a real close friend after all."

"Mm hmm. A man can't have too many friends. I had a real close friend in Colorado one time, but she died."

"What did she die of?" I asked.

"Distemper," he said.

Uncle Luden had brought presents from the unimaginable world beyond our mountains. My grandmother received a downy comforter and my mother a delicate black lace mantilla of Mexican handiwork. Johnson got a .22 pistol and my father a handsome 30-30 Marlin with a walnut stock. I got a series of presents, beginning with a real police detective badge and ending with a binocular contraption which showed a dozen or so inviting naked ladies inside. This last gift was commandeered by my father, who promised to return it to me when I got a little older. "That's provided I don't wear it out first," he said.

"Let me have a look in there," Johnson said. "Your Uncle Luden is a mighty sweet man."

"Heart of gold," my father said. "He could go anywhere in these hills and put up at anybody's house. But just for a couple of days."

"Wears em out, does he?"

"You watch who calls him on the telephone. First week or so it'll be one or two good old boys calling, and lots and lots of happy women. Then the voices will get deeper and louder and madder. That's the husbands and fathers and boyfriends. When it's all them and the last willing female voice has petered out, Luden starts dreaming about the great golden west again."

"Needs to smooth down a little," Johnson said. "Needs him a wife."

"I hope not," my father said. "He's already got three I know about."

"Three wives. Is he some kind of a Mormon?"

"He goes light on religion altogether. Told me he tried the Bible one time and couldn't pronounce the names."

"You don't reckon some husband might take and shoot him?"

"He's been awful lucky so far, but it's got to be a danger. . . That gives me an idea, though. I might come up with a little plan for us to try out."

"What kind of plan?"

"I'll tell you about it later."

Johnson held the peep show up to the sunlight and gave a sharp whistle. "Say, Joe Robert, have you seen this redheaded gal here?"

"With the green eyes?"

"Has she got eyes too?" Johnson asked.

"Let me see one time," I said.

"You'll have to wait till you're older and know your business," Johnson said.

I looked down at the battered toes of my brogans. That was going to be my whole destiny always, I thought. When I was as old as Ember Mountain they would still be keeping the important things from me. When I was ninety-nine years old and sitting on the porch in a rocking chair combing my long white beard, some towhead youngun would come up and ask, "What's it mean, grampaw, what is the world about?" And I would lean over and dribble tobacco spit into a rusty tin can and say, "I don't know, little boy. The sons of bitches never would tell me."

As Uncle Luden had a monarch reputation as a drinking man, Johnson and I were eager to see what he was like when he got drunk. We couldn't picture him wallowing about and throwing up, and I think that we secretly hoped that he gave away money when he was feeling mellow. Or perhaps he would behave no differently from Virgil Campbell, who simply watched the passing clouds and whistled and sang until sundown.

There were times we suspected he'd taken a nip or two, but we couldn't be sure because his demeanor hardly changed. His voice became deeper and had a breathy edge and he ambled along even slower than usual. But this was nothing remarkable and we were disappointed.

Then one morning he was drunk, and no mistake. He'd been out all night, "visiting friends," as he termed it, and the red panel truck came creeping up the road at about five miles per hour and wavered onto the shoulder and stopped, two wheels hanging off into the ditch.

Johnson and I were sitting on the front porch, sharpening the axes and scythes we'd need for the later season. Johnson watched the truck come up and, when it achieved its precarious roost on the roadside, murmured *Huh-oh* and gave me a knowing nod.

Nothing happened for a long time. Then the door opened and Uncle Luden struggled out of the cab on the passenger side and stood in the road, taking deep breaths and looking about as if he'd never seen this part of the United States before. He walked to the back and opened the door and got in, and this maneuver seemed to take a long time.

"Whoo-ee," Johnson said. "I can smell the ole whiskey on him from here, can't you, Jess?"

I nodded, though of course I couldn't smell anything.

The truck rocked back and forth and Uncle Luden plundered around and we could hear his muffled voice talking or singing, we couldn't tell which. When it fell silent for a space we thought maybe he'd crawled back into his traveling cot and gone to sleep, but then the back door opened again and Uncle Luden stepped down into the road and turned round three times slowly for all the universe to look at him. He was wearing a tall cowboy hat with a dented crown like Tim McCoy's and a Sam Browne belt over his pudgy chest and two fierce .45 pistols in tooled leather holsters riding his thighs. He stopped turning and looked up into the apex of the blue heavens and said "Wahoo" in a whispery melancholy monotone.

"Good Lord," Johnson said. "He's done turned into Gene Autry. What do you reckon he's going to do next?"

"I don't know," I said.

"I'm afraid I do," my grandmother said in the saddest

tone imaginable. We had been so interested in Uncle Luden that we hadn't heard her come out, didn't know she was there. She looked down at her son with an expression so mingled with tenderness and sorrow that I couldn't bear to watch her.

Uncle Luden returned to the back of the truck and came away with a cardboard box which he carried to the top of the hill and set down by the long board fence that used to enclose our hog lot there. With slow and painful care he began taking out of the box and arranging on the top board a row of little dimestone dolls, the cheap kind with painted eyes and gingham-scrap dresses. This took him a good while, as one or two of them would topple off while he was setting up another. Finally, though, he had twelve of them lined up and stepped back to survey his work.

"You know, that's a peculiar-looking sight," Johnson said, and at first I thought he meant Uncle Luden in his cowboy getup. But he meant the dolls, looking out of place and weirdly forlorn, perched on the warped rough board.

Uncle Luden walked from the fence into the road and turned and faced the dolls from a distance of about fifteen yards.

"If he's fixing to plug them dolls, he's got a chore," Johnson said. "He's too plumb cockeyed to hit a medium-size hill."

But he didn't miss. He drew the pistol from his right-hand holster with a smooth, easy motion and blew the first doll in line to plaster dust. Then he said in a firm voice, precisely articulating every syllable, *"We admitted we were powerless over alcohol, that our lives had become unmanageable."*

"What's he mean by that?" Johnson asked.

"Hush, Johnson," said my grandmother.

He raised the pistol again and, without seeming to take careful aim, pulverized the next doll with a single shot. *"Came to believe that a power greater than ourselves could restore us to sanity."*

And bang bang bang on down the line. He never missed a doll and after each shot would repeat one of what I later came to find out were the Twelve Steps of Alcoholics Anonymous. Having emptied one pistol, he switched to the other and was as expert with his left hand as with his right.

When the final doll was demolished he stood looking for a moment at the empty fence and then turned and came toward us. I thought he would be pleased with his marksmanship, but when he reached the porch I saw that his mouth was set in a hard sad line and his eyes under the low-pulled ten-gallon hat were dazed with trouble. He didn't speak to Johnson and me but pushed on by. He gave one brief watery glance at my grandmother and mumbled, "I'm sorry, Mother."

She brushed his shoulder lightly with the back of her hand. "Go on and take you some rest," she said. "I'll fix you something to eat in a little while."

He opened the kitchen door and inched it closed behind him.

"What I'm telling you is," Johnson said, "I don't never want him to get mad at me. You see what he done?"

"He can't get mad at ever a soul except just hisself," my grandmother said. There was a little smear of wet on her nose where a tear had leaked around the edge of her glasses.

Johnson and I might have dreamed the whole doll-shooting episode for all the difference it made in our lives. No one spoke of it, and Uncle Luden went on with his other concerns, which were manifold and mostly didn't include the rest of us.

He did include us in the reading of his mail, however. He had begun to receive letters as well as phone calls. These came in plain white envelopes without return addresses; the messages were printed in ugly capital letters on nondescript paper. I KNOW WHAT YOUR DOING YOU BETTER WACH OUT, the first one said.

After that, they began to come in twos and threes

every day, and each new message was more threatening than the last. LEAVE OUR WOMAN ALONE OR NOT LIVE LONG: that was one of the intermediate warnings. Not all the printing was in the same hand; there appeared to be a constituency of irate galoots out there in the hills who were handy to a carpenter's pencil and a mailbox.

He showed them around, smiling a silly half-smile, at first only bewildered, but beginning as the days went by to show signs of worry. "Who do you reckon would be sending me stuff like this?" he asked.

"I have no idea," my father said, "except maybe it's somebody who wants you to stay at home nights. If I got a letter like this one here, I might pause to think about it." With his fingertip he pushed across the tablecloth the paper that read KEEP YOUR TROWSERS BUTTENED AND SAVE YOUR LIFE.

"I ain't harming nobody," Uncle Luden said. "I don't go nowhere I ain't welcome."

"It's because you're so welcome that you get these letters."

"They don't scare me. I'm not going to change my plans."

"They would scare me," my father said.

Principal among Uncle Luden's plans was a picnic. He dearly loved picnics, Uncle Luden said, and he'd been thinking about eating fried chicken and rhubarb pie on top of Ember Mountain ever since he left Reno. He attacked preparations for this outing with meticulous thoroughness and sidereal slowness. He wanted to get the details orderly, he said, and this task took him a good three days. Finally Friday night arrived and he enjoined us all to be bright-eyed and bushy-tailed early next morning because we were headed up to Lickskillet Gap for an old-fashioned family picnic.

"That sounds wonderful, brother," my mother said. She liked anything having to do with *family*. If she heard there was a cockfight in hell, she'd favor it as long as the whole family was involved.

But when Uncle Luden said *bright and early* he didn't
mean when the sunshine was on the daisy. At 3:30 in the
morning we were jarred awake by a sound like a mountain falling. He had ignited a handful of firecrackers in a
steel ten-gallon milkcan he set in the stairwell. The windows rattled and the timbers throbbed.

"Get em up!" he said. "Whoever wants to picnic with
Luden Sorrells better get em up."

Johnson tumbled out of his tall wooden bed onto the
floor in his underwear. His hair was in spikes, and he
looked at me in wild alarm. "Good God!" he said. "Has
Hitler took and bombed us?"

I bounced gleefully. "It's Uncle Luden," I said, "waking
us up for the picnic."

We heard pistol shots and rushed to look out the narrow gable windows. Just as we looked a streak of pink-
orange fire zipped past, ascending to the stars; it was
lost for a moment, then burst into flower, a great Queen
Anne's lace of lucent blue and green and gold. We heard
far thuds.

"What's that?" I asked.

"Skyrocket," Johnson said. "Ain't it a honey?" His
blue eyes were bright as wet glass. "I wish your uncle
wouldn't be so all-fired secret about his picnic. You and
me might have slept through it."

Uncle Luden was already back in the house, herding
us along. "Get your clothes washed and your ears on," he
said.

Johnson and Uncle Luden went in the panel truck, my
father and mother and grandmother and I following in
our ramshackle Pontiac. My grandmother sat with me on
the ribbed felt upholstery in the back and I wondered
what she was thinking, but I couldn't see her face.
The four of us had fallen silent in the car, dislocated
perhaps by the early hour and by some other feeling I
couldn't name. Everything around us seemed strange and
we seemed strange inside it.

All the landscape fled away from us, only the stars followed. The dewy fields scored with barbwire, the nestled

cows and unmoving trees, the barns and sleeping houses, all spun by us like flipped pages. We went through the town of Tipton with its four lonesome stoplights and the Challenger paper mill smoking and rumbling even at this hour. We topped ridges and swooped into fog-patched bottoms, and then we were arrowing through the valley of the upper Pigeon on a straight road that bordered the oak shaded river. My uncle's red taillights drew us forward, and it might finally have been the stars that we were driving to.

We came to the mountain and the taillights swept around a curve and disappeared. The trees were closer around us now, a twisty tunnel of them, and our headlights washed over them and disturbed primeval sleep. The road ascended steadily and our old car strained on the grade.

Toward the top we caught up with Uncle Luden's car and followed him off the road into a grove, rolling easy over a ground soft with wet leaves and pine needles. In a clearing there we tumbled out and Johnson and my father set about building a fire; Uncle Luden stood near, taking no hand, but showing a most intense interest.

When the fire was blazing up, painting our faces orange, he went round to the other side to speak to my grandmother. "This used to be the place where old Turkey George would lay over on a hunting trip," he said.

She tried to see into the darkness. "I thought I kind of recognized it," she said. "Seems like it wasn't but a little piece from here that the Devoe youngun got snakebit and they had to pack him piggyback down the mountain."

Now they were talking about the old days and I moved away to watch Johnson build a smaller separate fire for the coffee. I didn't want to hear about the old days, the drab tragedies and the cruel rusties. Those mountain people of used-to-be seemed as alien to me as Siberians. When my grandmother talked to me about the old times, she seemed to be making it clear that I wouldn't have lasted long in that milieu.

Johnson laid an old piece of iron grating over the fire

and set the blue spatterware pot on top. My father enlisted me to help fry slabs of country ham at the other
fire, warning me not to let it cook too hard. "Just let the
ham get pink and the fat of it a little yellow," he said.
"Then it's done."

My mother had been frying eggs and now she went to
the other fire and dropped a handful of eggshell into the
coffee pot to settle the grounds. "Breakfast is just about
ready," she called cheerfully.

"We ain't set to eat just yet," Uncle Luden said and
went to his truck and returned with a tall red bottle
topped with gold foil. "Everybody has got to have some
of this California wine. Comes from up in Sonoma." He
opened it with the corkscrew of his fancy pocket knife
and poured a measure into each coffee cup.

It was the first wine of any sort I'd sipped and it has
lingered always in my mind. Wine still tastes for me of
the mountaintop of piny woods with a warm spring dawn
coming on, and that Spanishy word, *Sonoma*, is an exotic flavor all to itself.

Then we fell to eating. Day-old biscuits sweated in a
tin box by the fire and the hard-fried eggs and the ham
and boiled potatoes refried in ham grease. Coffee inky
and gritty, sweetened with molasses. We ate hunkered or
standing up, turning in slow pirouettes around the fires
to warm one side of our bodies and then the other.

We ate the end of night. The sky began to gray and the
stars gave up, flitted away one by one. The trees took
sharper shapes and the rocks and bushes began to show
clear.

Uncle Luden drifted apart, going to the outer edge of
firelight, a tin mug of coffee in one hand and a ham biscuit in the other. He turned and looked at us, lining us
up in his mind as if he were taking a souvenir photograph.
His small brown eyes were happy and grave, and he chewed
his biscuit and mustache indiscriminately.

My father nudged Johnson. "When that man dies," he
said, "and they cut him open, they'll find a hairball as
big as a pumpkin."

He finished his biscuit and coffee. He had picked out Johnson and me to stare at, rubbing his bulbous nose with a greasy finger. "I've had about all the breakfast I can stand," he said. "How about you boys?"

We agreed we'd had God's plenty. I felt as warm and full as a potbelly stove.

"Come on with me then up this way a piece," he said. "Something out here you might want to see."

We followed him from the clearing up a steep rooty path that wound between laurel thickets and beneath towering pines. He went along the path with surprising ease and alacrity, never drawing a hard breath, and Johnson and I were put on our mettle to keep up. Then the path seemed to end in a mazy screen of sawbriar and huckleberry. He parted it with some difficulty and we pushed through to a sudden high rock ledge overlooking a long valley.

First light sharpened the backbone edge of the eastern mountains. On this side toward us the flanks got darker at first, almost black, and the folds and ridges disappeared into that darkness. The valley looked frost-colored, though it was much too late for frost. The sun came on a little more and the mountainside colors shifted to deep mauve and then to purple and then to a hazy gray-blue. The greening valley floor was patched with ground fog and out of one of these patches rose a rope of silver smoke from a lone farmhouse kitchen.

The sun had got nearly to the tops of the far mountains and the light scalloped the broken edges, spilling toward us a flood of burning silver. The rocks around us began to hum and quiver and the birds began to clatter in the thickets. It was hard to look into that overbrimming furnace and I looked into the valley where the grass and trees were fast becoming green. Fog lay in the coves and hollers like puddles of bluejohn.

At last the sun had escaped the mountaintops and shone full upon Uncle Luden who stared into it wide-eyed; his arms were stretched out as if he were a fish hawk drying its feathers. He mumbled a little tune

I couldn't make out, but I could sense the sunlight
and blue air and the broad glory of morning soaking
into him. His slumped, pudgy body drank it all up like
thirsty sand.

Then he dropped his arms and blinked his eyes three
times and found the path. We followed him down through
the friendly woods and none of us said anything until we
were almost at the clearing. He stopped, blocking our
way, and said, "They got some mountains in California.
You ought to see them sometime. But it's not the same."
He marched on a few yards before halting again to de-
clare, "Some way or other, it just ain't the same."

We returned from our breakfast picnic about 9:30, hours
later than our usual milking time, and it seemed to me
that the cows in the lot gazed at us in sorrowful reproach.
My father and Johnson and I went to our chores, but
Uncle Luden stopped in only to change his shirt before
heading out again to new adventures.

"He must not be too clever at taking hints," my
father said. "If I started getting the kind of mail he does,
I wouldn't budge off this farm. Took me a long time to
think up those messages."

"Tonight's the night," Johnson said, but my father
shushed him.

"What's tonight?" I asked.

"Oh, nothing," Johnson said.

I asked my father. "What's tonight?"

He grinned. "Little pitchers have big ears," he said.

I'd heard that before, but I couldn't help touching my
ears to feel how enormous they had become. "Aw," I said.

In the afternoon there was a western wind and the sky
darkened. We returned from the long cornfield and got
rid of our evening chores at the barn under threat of rain.
Uncle Luden didn't return for supper and we ate in un-
accustomed quiet, as if we were only waiting for the im-
pending storm to loose its music.

Johnson and I went up at bedtime. In the dark I asked
him, "What's going to happen?" and he didn't answer.

"There ain't nothing going to happen," I said. "I'm going to go to sleep."

"That's the best idea," he said.

"There's something going to happen," I said, "and I want to know what it is." He didn't answer again and I determined that I would stay awake all night if I had to. I wasn't going to be left out. While I was deciding upon this plan, I fell asleep.

In the earliest morning I woke. The hour was violent with storm, lightning and thunder over our oak trees, lashings of rain rattling the gable windows by my bed. In the glare of blue lightning I saw that Johnson had risen and was putting on his clothes.

"What are you getting dressed for?"

"I got to go outside," he said.

"Outside? In this awful storm?"

"I heard Uncle Luden come up the stairs. He ought to be asleep by now. Just you keep quiet, you'll find out all about it." He stood up and adjusted himself, crossed to the door, and was lost in darkness.

It was hard to take in. I thought of Uncle Luden lying snug in bed, snoring through his whiskey, and of Johnson ranging out in the black downpour. Everybody's gone and lost their minds, I thought, unless it's some kind of rusty they didn't let me in on. That was the likeliest explanation, and I began to reflect bitterly once more about how they never let me know nothing.

Then I heard my father's unmistakable footsteps in the hall below. He paused at the bottom to cut on the lights and then ran up the stairs, his tread twice as loud and clumsy as necessary. By the time I got into my pants and out into the upstairs hallway, he was already pounding on Uncle Luden's bedroom door. Blam, blam. "Get up, Luden," he shouted. "They're here!"

"Who's here?" I said.

He turned his head and winked and put his finger to his lips. Then blam blam blam again. "Hurry up, Luden, for God's sake. They've come after you!"

"Who's come after him?" I said.

Blam blam. His pounding was as loud as the storm thunder.

It seemed hours before Uncle Luden opened the door. He was dressed in a long gray flannel nightshirt and had a strange little cap on his head, something like a miller's cap, but stained with decades of hair oil. His ruddy features were discomposed and his eyes were so bloodshot they looked like glowing embers. His words were thick and mushy when he spoke. "What's going on, Joe Robert? I was just getting good asleep."

"There's a bunch of men here to get you, Luden. God only knows what they mean to do."

From downstairs came the noise of a door slamming and an exaggerated tattoo of footsteps. A deep heavy voice called out, "Where's that lowdown polecat Luden Sorrells that's been messing with my woman?" He was trying to disguise it, but I recognized Johnson's voice, falsely hollow and deep.

"Oh Lord, they're in the house already," my father said.

Uncle Luden brightened. "I'll get my pistols," he said. "We can pick them off on the stairway."

"Leave those guns alone," my father said. "This posse is too many for us. We're going to have to hide you." He grabbed Uncle Luden by the shoulders and drew him out. "Quick, Jess, let's get him into your bedroom."

He shoved Uncle Luden through the door that I held open. I felt for the switch.

"*Don't* cut that light on! Are you crazy? Shut the door."

"Well, there ain't no place in here to hide," I said.

"There isn't?" My father sounded disappointed.

"No," I said. I'd tried to dodge my grandmother's chores a thousand times in this room and she'd scouted me out unfailingly.

The downstairs voice again, now muffled by the closed door so that it did sound convincingly strange: *"Where's he at? I'll make mincemeat out of that Luden Sorrells!"*

"Get over to the window, Luden," my father said. "We'll

hide you up on the roof." He dragged him along and thrust open the window. Just as he did, there was a monster slash of lightning and a carom of thunder and the oak limbs thrashed.

"It's raining," Uncle Luden observed. "I ain't going out in that."

"Better water than buckshot," my father said. "Hurry up now. I already hear them on the stairs."

"Get me my pistols and I'll drop the lot of them."

"Not with Jess here. You wouldn't want him to get hurt. Slide on out and climb up by the chimney. They won't look out the window."

There was a rapping at the bedroom door. *"I'll learn that Luden Sorrells to tomcat."*

He stood a moment in wild indecision, then squirreled through the window pretty deftly. My father slammed it shut and latched it. Then there was Uncle Luden's face mashed flat against the glass. He looked like a drugged catfish, and he mouthed a single word we couldn't hear but which I knew profoundly by heart: *Wahoo.* My father motioned for him to get away from the window and climb to the ridgepole. He made an apoplectic grimace and was gone.

My father went to the door and opened it for Johnson whose face was distorted by the world's broadest grin. "Did it work?" he asked.

"Like clockwork," my father said.

"He went out the window?"

"Yes."

"He's up on the rooftop?"

"Yes."

"In this rainstorm?"

"Yes."

Johnson began laughing then at last. His ordinarily red face heated to an inhuman scarlet. Tears squeezed out of his blue eyes and he hugged his stomach. He leaned against the wall and then slid down it until he was sitting flat on the floor. Laughter racked his torso like electric shock, and finally he was lying flat on his back in the hallway, whooping and drumming his heels.

My father hardly smiled. He was dazzled by the precision of the joke. "Like clockwork," he said. "It went off as slick as a greased weasel." He stood there overcome by awe of his own genius.

"Are you going to leave him on the roof?" I asked.

"No-no, we'll get him down in a minute," my father said. "But we've got an important decision to make first. Are we going to tell him it's a rusty or are we going to let him keep on thinking there's a posse of jealous menfolks?"

"He'll drown to death out there," I said. "He'll get struck by lightning."

Johnson was sitting up, only giggling now, and rubbing his ribs. "Oh, let's *tell* him," he said. Then the laughter laid him out flat again.

A few days more and it was time for Uncle Luden to depart. We had decided it would be too cruel to let him in on the trickery, so he had stopped drinking entirely and at night went no more a-roving. He sat with us at the dining table until the coffee grew cold and the pork dripping congealed on the plates. Then he would sit with us on the long porch to watch the night wind among the stars, to see the fanciful Cecropia moths flatten against the window screens. He refused to answer the telephone. "Peace and quiet, that's what a man wants," he said. "Whoever calls, tell them I ain't to be found."

"What if it's little old Spanky-Sue?" my father asked.

"Mm hmm." He chewed his mustache. "Tell her I have become a religious hermit and am living in a cave with an owl."

"You reckon that'll satisfy her?"

"Well," he said, "there ain't no way to *satisfy* her."

Next morning he began lugging his brandy and bourbon and muscatel empties out to the trash pile. That was just the first step, and it actually took him two more

46

days to pack and square away. No one offered to aid him, not even when my mother remonstrated. "I'd help him pack if I wanted him to leave," my father replied, and she smiled dimly and said no more.

When he mounted the running board to get in and drive away, he was wearing white flannel pants supported by wide leather suspenders and a red and green plaid shirt with a yellow silk vest open over it. Pulled low over his eyes was a green eyeshade. "I been thinking I might stop off on the way and play me a hand of poker," he said.

"That's the way," Johnson said. "You'll clean them cowboys out. You won't leave em boots to walk home in."

The women hugged and kissed him and Johnson and my father and I shook his hand, not looking into his face. Still standing on the running board he uttered again in the same low breathy voice his melancholy war cry. "Wahoo." Then he settled himself behind the wheel and looked through the windshield down the crooked dirt road as if it were a straight shot into infinity. Then he pressed the starter.

Three / **The Beard**

Uncle Gurton's beard had a long and complex history, but I will try not to bore us with much of that. Enough to say that it was a fabled beard and that when my father and I heard that Uncle Gurton was coming to visit we were thrilled at the prospect of viewing the legendary fleece.

"How long is that beard of his now?" my father asked my grandmother.

She smiled a secret smile. "Oh, I wouldn't have no idea," she said. "But he's been growing it for forty years or more and ain't once yet trimmed it. That's what I hear tell."

"And he's coming here to our house to visit?" I asked.

"That's what Aunt Sary says in her letter." She held up the scrawled bit of paper, but not close enough for us to read the writing.

"And when is he going to get here?"

"She wouldn't know about that. You'll just have to wait."

"Hot damn," my father said. "If this ain't the biggest thing since Christmas. We're going to make that old man plenty welcome."

"Now, Joe Robert, don't you be deviling Uncle Gurton," she said. "Leave him in peace."

"Oh, I wouldn't harm a hair of his face," he said. "When you say he's coming?"

She smiled again. "You'll just have to wait till he shows up."

Show up is exactly what Uncle Gurton did. We heard no car or truck arrive, and he didn't walk into the house or knock at the door. One Tuesday noon he was just there, standing under the walnut tree in the side yard and staring at our chopblock and pile of kindling as if he'd never seen such objects upon the face of the earth. An apparition, he simply became present.

The three of us raised our heads from our dinner plates at the same time and saw him, and a spooky feeling came over us.

"What in the world is *that?*" my father asked.

"Uncle Gurton," said my grandmother in her serenest voice.

His back was toward us, so that all we could tell was that he was a very tall man, his white head bare, and dressed in faded overalls and a green plaid shirt, as lean and narrow as a fence rail, and warped with age and weather. Then, as if presenting himself formally to our gaze, he turned around.

I was profoundly disappointed. The famous beard that he had been working on for forty years and more, the beard that was the pivot of so many stories, was tucked down inside his overalls bib.

My father and I had made bets whether it would hang down to his belly button or all the way down to his knees, and now we couldn't say.

But even apart from his beard he was an extraordinary-appearing person. His arms were too long for his shirt sleeves and his hands dangled out like big price tags. His overalls legs were too short and his skinny legs went naked into his high-topped brogans. His long hair was white and hung down both sides of his ruddy sharp-featured face. The beard, as purely white as a morning cloud, went down behind his overalls bib, and what happened to it after that, what it truly looked like, only Uncle Gurton and the almighty and omniscient God could say.

"Jess," my grandmother said, "go out and welcome Uncle Gurton to the house."

"Please, ma'am, no," I said. Uncle Gurton was too famous in my mind. It would have been easier to shake hands with Lou Gehrig.

"He does look kind of fearsome," my father said. "I'll go gather him in."

He went out and talked and Uncle Gurton gave him one short nod and then they came into the house. When the old man entered our small alcove dining space he looked even taller and odder than he had outdoors. His head nearly scraped the low ceiling.

My grandmother told him how glad we were to see him and how we hoped he would stay a long time, and asked him to sit and eat with us. Which he did with right good will. She brought flatware and a glass of buttermilk and a plate piled full of green beans, cornbread, and fried rabbit. Then she sat down at the end of the table and began to question him.

"How is Aunt Jewel getting along?" she asked.

Uncle Gurton smiled and was silent.

She waited a space of time and asked, "How is Cousin Harold doing?"

He gave her a smile as warm and friendly as the first, and as informative as a spoon.

In a while she lit on the correct form. "Has Hiram Williams got him a good tobacco crop set out?" He smiled and gave a vigorous affirmative shake of his head. After this, she asked questions that could be answered yes or no, and Uncle Gurton would nod a cheerful Yes or wag a downcast No.

And all during this exchange he was feeding voraciously. Great heaping forkfuls went into his hirsute mouth with mechanical accuracy and rapidity. A sight awesome to behold. My father kept filling his plate and Uncle Gurton kept emptying it. My father described it later: "The way he was forking at it, and with all that hair around his mouth, I kept thinking it was a man throwing a wagonload of alfalfa into a hayloft."

He finished by downing a whole glass of buttermilk. We came to find out that buttermilk was his sole beverage, breakfast, dinner, supper. He never touched anything else, not even water.

He edged his chair back from the table.

"Uncle Gurton, won't you have a little something else?" my grandmother asked.

"No thank you," he said. "I've had an elegant sufficiency; any more would be a superfluity."

That was his one saying, the only one we ever heard him utter, and he was as proud of it as another man might be of a prize beagle. He said this sentence at the end of every meal, and we came to realize that he got mighty upset, his whole day was lusterless, if you didn't ask him to have a little more something, and give him occasion to say his sentence.

My father's mouth flew open like a phoebe's after a fly. His eyes lit up with surprise. "Would you mind saying that again, Uncle Gurton?" he asked. "What you just said?"

Uncle Gurton gave him a sweet warm smile and disappeared.

I don't mean that he dissolved into nothingness before our watching eyes like a trick ghost in a horror movie. But he evaded my father's request with one of those silent smiles, and when we had got up and scraped our dishes into the slop bucket and stacked them on the drainboard of the sink and turned around, Uncle Gurton was gone. His chair was angled back from the table, his red and white checked napkin folded neatly and laid in the seat, and he was nowhere to be seen. If it weren't for the soiled plate with the knife and fork primly crossed and the empty streaked glass, we might not have believed that he had been there. No footsteps of departure, no sound of the side door, nothing.

"Our Uncle Gurton has got some interesting ways about him," my father said.

"Poor old soul," my grandmother murmured.

This habit of absenting and distancing himself we learned to know as an integral part of Uncle Gurton's character, as one with the man as his silence. You would sight him on the ridge of the pasture above the farther barn, his stark figure scarecrowlike against the sky and leaning into the wind, and then if you glanced off into the pear tree to see a bluejay, he was no longer on the ridge when you looked again. Snuffed out of the present world like a match flame. Translated into another and inevitable dimension of space. What? Where? When was he? He was an enigma of many variations, and his one answer, silence, satisfied them all as far as he was concerned.

"There's one thing, though, you can be certain of," my father said. "He won't miss a mealtime."

And this was true. As soon as the first steaming dish of corn or squash or squirrel burgoo was set out, Uncle Gurton *arrived* from whatever mystery world otherwise absorbed him.

My father kept testing him. "Uncle Gurton," he said, "this afternoon Jess and me have got a little fence mending to do along the back side of the far oatfield. Restring some barbwire, reset a few posts. How'd you like to go along and keep us company?"

There was the smile, sweet and friendly and utterly inscrutable.

My father rephrased the question. "I mean," he said, "would you be willing to go along with us, maybe lend a hand?"

Uncle Gurton nodded.

My father leaned back in his chair. "That's fine," he said. "We'll go catch us a smoke out on the porch here after lunch and then we'll go on over to the oatfield."

What distracted us? When we finished eating and tidied up a bit, Uncle Gurton was gone again. The folded napkin, the crossed knife and fork; and no Uncle Gurton.

"I'm going to get me a moving picture camera," my father said. "Because I want to find out how he does that. I believe that it's a truly rare gift that he has."

He pondered the matter all the way out to the fence line, the roll of barbwire hoisted on his shoulder and bouncing on the burlap-sack pad with every stride. I walked at his side, toting the awkward posthole diggers and the wire stretcher. "I put the question to him wrong," he said at last. "I didn't ask him was he actually going to go with us, but was he *willing* to go."

"What's the difference?" I said.

"He was willing to go, all right, but he was even more willing not to."

At the top of the high second hill of the pasture we turned to look back. There in the dusty road between the house and the first barn, as steady as a mailbox post, stood Uncle Gurton.

I dropped the posthole diggers with a loud clatter. When we looked again, the road was empty.

"No, a movie camera wouldn't capture it," my father said. "It would take some kind of invention that is beyond the capacity of present-day science."

We were resting from the fence work. We sat in the shade of a big red oak and watched the wind write long cursive sentences in the field of whitening oats.

"One question we don't need to ask," my father said. "Whether he sleeps with his beard inside or outside the covers. Stands to reason that a man who would tuck his beard down in his overalls will sleep with it under the covers."

"How long do you reckon it is?" It was the thousandth time I had asked that question.

"Before he got here, I would've guessed it was a foot and a half," he said. "And then when I saw him first,

I'd've said two feet. But now the more I don't see it the longer it gets. I've been imagining it four or five feet easy."

"You really think it's all that long?"

"I've got to where I'll think anything when it comes to that beard."

"If it's that long he has to let it run down his britches leg," I said. "Which one you think, left or right?"

"Kind of a ticklish decision," he said. "Maybe he divides it up, half down one leg, half down the other."

"You reckon it's the same color all over?"

He gave me a level look. "Jess, for anything I know, it's green and purple polka-dotted under them overalls and he's got it braided into hangnooses. But I'll tell you what. I'm bound and determined to see that beard, every inch of it. I'll never sleep easy again till I do."

"How are you going to do that?"

"I'll let you know."

It was three days later, the hour before suppertime, when he revealed his grand and cunning design. He took a thumb-sized blue bottle out of his pocket. "You see this? This is our beard-catcher; this is going to turn the trick."

"What is it?"

"It's a sleeping draught I got from Doc McGreavy."

Doc McGreavy was our veterinarian, an old man who lived with his wife in a dark little house three miles from us, at the very end of the road where the mountainside pines took possession and human habitation left off.

"What are you going to do?"

"Slip it in his buttermilk. When he goes to bed he'll sleep as sound as a bear wintering in. Then we'll have us a look at that beard."

"You think it'll work?"

"Doc says it'll lay a horse down, he's put many a horse to sleep with it. I'll give Uncle Gurton just a little bit. We won't be hurting him any."

"You sure?"

He was impatient. "Sure I'm sure."

And so at supper my father kept close watch on Uncle Gurton's buttermilk. When he had drunk off the first glass, my father picked it up. "Here," he said, "let me get you some more, Uncle Gurton." He tipped me an evil wink and I knew he was going to drop the powders.

Uncle Gurton nodded and flashed the friendliest smile in his smile box, and when the buttermilk came he drained it in two swallows. My father looked so gleeful I was afraid he'd bust out laughing and spoil it all.

Then I was afraid he'd got hold of the wrong powders because nothing seemed to be happening. Uncle Gurton was as bright eyed silent as ever and was forking into the stewed tomatoes with devastating effect. But in a few minutes I saw that his eyes were growing faraway cloudy and the lids were drooping.

"Have another piece of cornbread," my father suggested.

"No thank you," he said. "I've had an elegant suffi-ciency—"

But he didn't say on to *the superfluity* and we knew we had him. He rose from the table and stumbled through the kitchen and out the door, headed down the hall for the stairway. He didn't cross his knife and fork on the plate, and the checked napkin lay on the floor where he'd dropped it. My father retrieved it and laid it by his plate.

My grandmother followed his progress with curious eyes. "Uncle Gurton is right strange-acting. I wonder is he feeling poorly."

"Aw, he's okay," my father said. "He's just plumb tuck-ered from appearing and disappearing out of thin air all day."

We cleaned and stacked our dishes and then retired to the side porch where my father smoked his cigarette after meals.

"We going to see the beard now?" I asked.

"Better give him a little while, make sure he's sound asleep. Let's go out to the shed a minute."

In the woodshed he took a dusty kerosene lantern off a hook and shook it to hear if there was oil in the reservoir. He reached an old motheaten blue sweater off a nail and wiped the cobweb off the lamp. "We'll need this if we're going to be good and sneaky," he said. He brought the lamp and the sweater and we returned to the porch and he smoked two slow cigarettes and we watched the first stars pierce the western sky. The far hills went hazy blue and then purple-black.

"Let's go," he said, and we opened the forbidden door and tiptoed through the dark sun parlor. The souvenir teacups rattled on the glassed-in shelves. It was stale in here and dusty. I was afraid I'd sneeze and trumpet our crime to the world at large.

We entered into the dark stairway hall and stood for a moment to listen. My father struck a kitchen match with his thumbnail and lit the wick and let the shell down. The pale orange light made our shadows giant on the walls, and everything was strange in here in the hallway, all silent, and in the stairwell above in the hovering darkness. I felt a way I'd never felt before, like a thief or a detective. My breath was quick, the pulse tight in my temples.

We climbed the stairs one careful step at a time. Our shadows fell behind us and washed up on the far wall and the shadows of the banister posts spun like ghostly wheel spokes. My father held the lantern by his side in his left hand and I hid in his righthand shadow, moving when he did.

We paused at the top of the stairs and he raised the lantern. The door to Uncle Gurton's room was at the end of the hall and we edged toward it. Every snap and squeak of the floor made me fearful; I was certain we'd be discovered. What could we say to Uncle Gurton or my grandmother when they found us? I realized, maybe for the first time, that my father wasn't always the safest protection in the world.

At that fateful door we stopped and held our breaths to listen. My father began to ease the door open, turning the knob slowly, slowly, until it ceased and the door swung open upon blackness. We heard the sound of heavy breathing and I felt relieved to know we hadn't poisoned the old man to death. My father had wrapped the wool sweater around the lantern and now he rolled it up from the bottom, showing a little light at a time.

We needn't have been so precisely stealthy. Uncle Gurton's mouth was open and, lying flat on his back, he uttered a gurgling half-snore. We could have dropped a wagonload of tin kettles on the floor and he wouldn't have stirred an ounce.

I was impressed by how Uncle Gurton lived. There were a few shirts on hangers in the open closets and one shirt hung on the back of a chair by the foot of the bed. In front of this chair his battered brogans sat, a sock dangling out of the top of each. And that was all I saw there. He led a simple existence.

My father handed me the lantern and we advanced to the edge of the bed. After giving me one significant and thrilling glance, he began to turn the sheet down from under the old man's chin. We were dismayed to discover that Uncle Gurton slept in his overalls. He wore no shirt; his naked freckled arms lay flat beside him, but the blue denim bib still hid what we had schemed so anxiously to disclose. My father rolled the sheet down to Uncle Gurton's waist, then leaned back from the bedside.

He gave me another look, this one of bewilderment and frustration. Little beads of sweat stood on his forehead. I shrugged. I was ready to leave, figuring Uncle Gurton was just one too many for us. He was a coon we couldn't tree.

But we'd come too far for my father to let it go. He reached and unhooked the gallus on the far side; then loosed the one nearer. Then he inched the bib down.

We were not disappointed; it was everything we had come to see. A creeklet of shining white lay over Uncle Gurton's skinny chest and gleamed in the lantern light like a drawer of silver spoons. It was light and dry and immaculately clean—a wonder because we'd never known Uncle Gurton to bathe. We'd never seen him do much but eat.

I thought the beard was marvelous, and I couldn't regret all our trouble and terror. It was like visiting a famous monument—Natural Bridge, Virginia, say; and I felt a different person now I'd seen it.

But the great question went begging. How long was it? We couldn't tell, and there didn't seem to be any way to find out unless we stripped him naked or tugged the beard to light by handfuls.

We stood gazing dejected until the beard began to move. It was a movement hard to distinguish. At first I thought it was flowing away to the foot of the bed like a brook, and then I thought it was rising like early mist over a pond. My father clutched my shoulder and I knew he saw this motion too.

Then suddenly it was out upon us, billow on billow of gleaming dry wavy silver beard, spilling out over the sheet and spreading over the bed like an overturned bucket of milk. It flowed over the foot of the bed and then down the sides, noiseless, hypnotic. There was no end to it.

I felt it stream over my shoe tops and round my ankles and it was all I could do to stifle a shriek. I dropped the lantern and my father bent and picked it up before it could set fire to the beard, to the house. We retreated, stepping backward quickly, but always facing the bed. We were afraid to turn our backs on that freed beard.

Now over Uncle Gurton's torso it began to rise into the air, mounding up dry and white and airy. It was like seeing a frosty stack of hay rising of its own volition out of the ground. Little streamers of beard detached from the mass and began to wave in the air like the antennae of butterflies. They searched around the tall flat headboard of the bed and went corkscrewing up the curtain drawstrings. In just a moment the beard had curled in and out, around and over, the chair in the middle of the floor like wisteria overtaking a trellis.

At last my father said something, speaking out loud. *My God*, was what he said.

"Let's please leave," I said. The flow of beard was up to my calves now and I was afraid it would start wrapping around my legs the way it had gone over the chair. Then what would happen?

"Go on," my father said. "I'm right behind you." Then he pointed and said *My God* again.

Over the bed the beard had climbed until it was like a fogbank, only more solid, and threatened to topple forward. But it was still sliding underneath in sheets off the bed like a small waterfall, and now out of that misty mass and down over the edge of the bed came a birchbark canoe with two painted Cherokee Indians paddling with smooth alacrity. Above them, out of the mist-bank of beard, flew a hawk pursued by a scattering of blackbirds. We heard a silvery distant singing and saw a provocative flashing and then a mermaid climbed out of the beard and positioned herself in the streaming-over straight chair. She did not seem to see my father and me, but gazed into some private distance and sang her bell-like song; the hair that fell over her shoulders, hiding her breasts, was the same color as Uncle Gurton's beard.

Behind the mermaid's singing all sorts of other sounds emerged, squeaks and squawks, chatterings, chitterings, muffled roars, howls, and thunderings: the background noises in a Tarzan movie. In the corner of the room was a sudden and terrific upheaval and a great mass of beard lifted to the height of the ceiling, then subsided to ominous silence. We glimpsed the movement of a huge indistinct bulk beneath the surface, moving stately-swift toward the far wall.

"What's that?" I whispered.

My father said *My God* once more and then murmured, "I believe to my soul it's a damn big white whale."

"I really think it's time to get out of here."

"I do believe you're absolutely right, Jess," he said. He

pointed at three dark sharp triangles cutting through the surface. "Sharks in here too. Well, that settles that. We'd better go, I reckon."

He slipped the lantern bail up over his shoulder and dropped the old wool sweater. It floated for a moment on the surface of the silver hair and suddenly submerged. Something had snatched it under, I didn't want to know what.

We made our way to the door, lifting our feet high, and after a minute of straining together, managed to push the slowly closing door against the wall. The river of beard was already out into the upper hall, spreading both ways along the corridor. We stopped at the top of the stairs and my father unslung the lantern from his shoulder and held it up. The beard was flowing steadily down the steps, and the footing on the stairway looked plenty treacherous.

"What do you think?" I asked.

"I don't know. I don't trust it."

"I know what," I said. "Let's slide down the banister."

"Yeah, that's the ticket," he said. "I'll go first and hold the lantern for you. You can see your way down better."

"I'll go first."

"Stay right here and watch if I get down okay." He clenched the tin wire bail in his teeth. Then he straddled and lifted his feet and slid to the bottom pretty nifty. But he hit the newel post there hard and I knew if he hadn't had a mouthful of lantern bail I'd have heard some hair-singeing curses. He got off and stepped back, holding the lantern with one hand and rubbing his ass with the other. "Come on," he said, "you can make it just fine."

But as I was getting set to mount the banister, my left foot tangled in a wavelet of beard and I pitched forward. I was sure I was drowned or strangled, but my right hand on the banister held me up and I twisted over and got hold with my left hand and pulled myself up. Then I got on and slid down.

"I was worried about you for a second there," he said. "Come on, let's go."

"I was a little worried myself."

60

The beard was only shoe top deep down here and we went padding through it into the little sitting room, then through the kitchen hallway and out the back door.

In the yard stood a startling black apparition, but when my father held the lantern toward it, it was only my grandmother standing straight and narrow and angry in a wine-colored bathrobe. "What have you boys been doing?" she asked.

We said nothing and turned to look at the house. The upstairs windows were packed solid white with beard, and there were trailers coming out of the downstairs kitchen windows, and from the chimney a long flame-like banner of it reached toward the stars and swayed in the cold breeze.

"We just wanted to see Uncle Gurton's beard," I told her.

She clucked her tongue. "Well, do you think you've seen enough of it?"

My father looked at her and gave a deep and mournful sigh. "Yes ma'am," he said. "I've seen an elegant sufficiency. Any more—" He choked on a giggle like a bone in his throat. "Any more would be a superfluity."

Four / *The Change of Heart*

I have some difficulty describing my father's attitude toward religion. Let us say that he was tolerant, and whatever private ideas he entertained about divinity and the related mysteries he kept private. This was fairly unusual behavior in our part of the country. The hills around us were full of loud primitive denominations of every strange stripe, whose members proclaimed their beliefs at any public opportunity. If proclamation seemed not to persuade a skeptical listener, those zealots importuned; if importuning failed, they badgered.

My father was untroubled. His was a quizzical attention, and the enthusiasm of the gospel shouters amused him. "What are they so het up about?" he asked. "If what they believe is correct, they've got it made. If they really believed everything they said, they wouldn't have to say it so much."

"They just want to share the joys of eternity with you, Brother," Johnson Gibbs said.

"How do they know I'm not saved? I might be."

"If you're saved," Johnson said, "you're keeping it mighty secret. You want to riproar about it and carry on, and not leave folks in the dark."

"Maybe I'll do that," he said. "I might have a gift for riproaring."

But what didn't much bother my father was a soreness and a tribulation to Virgil Campbell. Mr. Campbell sat in his little grocery store by the iron bridge where Trivet Creek poured into Pigeon River, drinking the whiskey he craved when he felt like it, and swearing soul-daunting oaths just to pass the hours. These habits made him an easy target for the Ugly Holies; for here he was, a gilt-edge bona fide sinner right out in open daylight who was keeping not the least little one of his vices hidden. It must have seemed to the proselytizers that Satan was saying, "Behold my prize champion, boys. Step up and take your best lick."

They weren't about to hang back. If it wasn't a scrawny jackleg preacher leaning on the greasy chopblock to sermonize the hapless pudgy man, then it was some long jawed deacon. If it wasn't a deacon, then it was a fierce-talking sister of the church, her gray hair pinned back, gray light glinting on her rimless spectacles. Not even the children gave him peace. Their parents had taught them to say, after paying for their Kool-Aid or peppermints, "Thank you kindly, Mr. Bound-for-Hell."

He had a sense of irony and told my father that he'd come goddam near changing the name of his establishment to the Bound for Hell Grocery & Dry Goods and only backed off when he found out what it would cost to have his sign repainted.

And then Johnson Gibbs had lost that baseball game Mr. Campbell got up against the True Light Rainbow Baptist Church. "That was a trial," he said. "There wasn't one car on the road didn't stop here for somebody to run in and tell me how I backed the wrong team because I ain't sitting on the righthand side of Jesus."

"I'd be more inclined to fault Johnson's pitching," my father said.

"Suppose I'd been sitting on the sunny side of the Lord and we won that game. Where would that put *them*?" Mr. Campbell said.

"Might have started a theological ruckus."

"They can't stand much more ruckus," he said. "There where the road starts up Turkey Cove is your Rainbow

Baptist Church, and it's a nice white wood church. You go on up the cove a piece and there's a little old concrete block house which is your New Rainbow Baptist Church. A big chunk of them busted away in an argument over predestination. Another two miles is the True Light Rainbow Baptist Church, which starts off with a few concrete blocks and finishes up tar paper siding."

"And if we'd won that baseball game?"

"They'd of had them another fight. You'd go up on the mountain and find a pup tent by the road. The One True Light Rainbow Reformed Holiness Baptist Church of the Curveball Jesus."

"Too bad we didn't win," my father said. "I'd be curious to read the articles of faith of that one."

The enthusiast who gave Mr. Campbell most trouble was a green eyed crooked-toothed skinny fellow named Canary. Famous for the virulence of his righteousness, he had been asked to uncongregate himself from a couple of the more easy-going churches. He told Mr. Campbell flat out that he was a wicked sight on the face of the earth and a stink unto the nostrils of heaven. He told Mr. Campbell that every day.

"I'm getting right sick of it, Joe Robert," he said to my father. "He stops by here once a day for two months now to say that stuff, and so far he ain't bought the first saltine."

"Kind of wearisome," my father said.

Mr. Campbell nodded. "We all got our cross to bear," he said.

Eight days later we encountered this man Canary in Mr. Campbell's store. He frightened me a little. It was obvious that a wild passion animated his gangly frame. His motions were quick and jerky and when he talked flecks of spit sprayed from his lips, gleaming like sparks. He talked a lot. When my father and I entered he was already perorating Mr. Campbell, looming over him like a rickety windmill, flapping his arms like broken wings.

He was telling Mr. Campbell how he would burn forever in hell. "Can you think what it'll be like, Brother Campbell? No, you can't start on that job. You might-a burned your hand on the stove one time and thought that hurt you some. Made you jerk your hand right away. But, Brother Campbell, that wasn't nothing to what you're going to feel. That wasn't the least little bit of it. Because it'll be that and a hundred times worser and it won't never let up. You'll be praying for water and the devil will bring you brimstone. You'll be hollering for a breath of cool air and he'll be carrying you buckets of coals. You'll be calling on Jesus then, Brother, calling out the blessed name of our Savior and it won't do you no good. Jesus will done've turned His back on you then. It'll make Him sorry to do it, there'll be tears in His precious eyes, but it'll be too late and you'll have to stay where you're at, and you ain't going to like it there. The Book promises you won't like it there."

Mr. Campbell's face turned scarlet and the edges of his lips white. But he wasn't going to say anything; he fortified himself, clenched like a fist, like a rock in the wind, not to be swayed, not to be angered. We could see that he was going to resist in silence, and silent resistance must have been torture for him, so counter to his nature that this present situation would be his hell, and not any burning pit.

Canary knew his advantage. "But they's a way, Brother Campbell," he said, "they's a way out of it for you. If you'll just turn to Jesus right now, turn to Him right now this very minute and hour, and accept the Lord as your own personal savior, then you won't never see the inside of hell and not even the sorry gates of it. If you'll turn to Jesus right this minute and get down on your knees and accept Him as your personal savior, why then you'll know peace and goodness forever and be with the saints in heaven. You don't have to take my word for it, Brother, it's all right there in the Book. And you won't never regret it, Brother. You'll become like a little child."

My father stepped apart from me then and took three long strides up the aisle. He stopped beside the chopblock and raised his hands above his head and trembled them like poplar leaves. "Canary!" he cried out in a voice so deep and rich I almost couldn't recognize it as his.

The skinny man turned. His expression was startled and his voice quiet when he said, "Yessir, what can I do for you?"

"Canary!" my father said again, louder this time. "I have beheld you in a vision!"

He blinked. "What you say now?"

"The Lord God Almighty appeared to me in a vision," my father said. "In the deep night he spoke of you, Canary, so as to give my heart grievous trouble. He said unto me that there was a man Canary traipsing about the county meddling into the concerns of other folks. The Lord spoke unto me saying, This man Canary is not to be trusted. He is using my name in vain, the Lord told me, to poke his snout where it's got no business. The Lord told me that this man Canary calls himself My servant but he's not My servant and he has got an ungrateful heart. Yes, an ungrateful heart, the Lord told me, because he ought to be on his knees all he can, thanking Me that somebody hasn't busted his nose for him, thankful that some godly and modest man hasn't grabbed a meat cleaver and chopped off his runty little old pecker. It was you He showed me in the vision, Canary, and that's how I came to recognize you. And in this vision the good Lord also allowed me to see the meat cleaver. It was floating in the air in front of me, just like the wheel the prophet Ezekiel saw. This was a true vision that God gave to me and I could see all things as clear as daylight. That meat cleaver I came to see in my vision is this very one here on this chopblock." And he stretched forth his hand and picked up the greasy old cleaver there and hefted it.

Canary turned a little pale. "I don't know who you are, Brother," he said, "but I think you must have had a false vision. The devil is full of tricks that can fool a man."

"This was a true vision," my father said sternly, "and not to be made mock of. There is a voice in my head right now, telling me that I was visited by no idle vision but by a prophecy that would come true in the fullness of time." He struck the cleaver into the edge of the block and bore down and cracked off a chip.

"I'll be going along now," Canary said. "I don't believe in that vision you talk about, but I don't believe in violence neither. I ain't afraid of you, but I don't believe in violence."

He didn't try to squeeze down the aisle by my father, though. He sidled along the other side of the table of cloth goods and around behind the bins of bolts and nails.

"That's right, Canary," he said. "Never fear any man. Fear only the wrath that is to come."

Canary opened the door without seeming to open it and was gone out into the twilight without seeming to retreat.

Mr. Campbell laughed a while. Then he said, "Now, Joe Robert, what if he'd tried to take the meat knife away from you?"

He laid it gently on the block. "That wasn't in the vision," he said.

But when my grandmother heard about the incident she wasn't pleased a whit. "Making fun of somebody's religion," she said. "That ain't no way. That's a right trashy way to act."

"I don't mind his religion," my father said. "I was just aiming to take a little heat off Virgil. I think he'd stood about as much as he was going to. Hell, I might have saved that old Canary's hide."

"Listen at you swear," she said. She rapped him on a knuckle with her thimble.

But he went on. "Anyway, how do you know I didn't have a vision just like I said? These hillside Holies are always talking to Jesus in person. Why wouldn't He talk to me? Maybe He'd rather talk to me. They're not the most entertaining company in the world."

She laid his green shirt that she was mending across the dining room table. "You ain't never had no vision," she said. "You ain't never had no talk with God. You ain't the kind that does."

I felt a bit of a shiver between my shoulder blades. It was clear that she'd had a vision, she had truly talked with God; she simply didn't noise the fact around, calling attention to herself. Many questions came into my mind to ask her, but I knew she wouldn't answer. She would just tell me to spend more time on my knees at my bedside. There never would be a right time to ask her, and I never did.

My father was abashed at this judgment. "I'm as good as the next man," he said. "Who's to say God favors that Canary over me? God might take a notion to talk to me any minute now."

"You wouldn't know how to hear," she said. She gave him one of her shriveling glances through the square-edged spectacles. "You got a good heart, Joe Robert, nobody's got a better. But you ain't come to serious manhood yet. You ain't ready for any meeting with your Lord. You are too flibberty and not contrite."

He hung his head before her like a little boy, and I couldn't tell whether he was teasing or not.

My grandmother was not privy to the mind of God, and her information about this subject was faulty. I came to find out over the years that much of her wisdom was unsound, but when she propounded no one questioned. My grandmother drew deference from a person as handily as a crowbar draws nails from a post. Maybe it was her cheerfully aged face and tall angular frame and her way of staring, when she intended to impress, directly at the bridge of your nose.

Nevertheless, she was flat wrong, for eleven days later God spoke to my father.

In fact, He spoke to all three of us.

Johnson Gibbs and my father and I were mucking out the milking stalls in the lower barn. Ours was a primitive milking arrangement; we had no concrete floor, only bare earth spread with straw. It was supremely unsanitary, and our milk had to be sold as Grade C for measly profit. We were going to pour concrete when we got the money, but we never got the money.

It was a chore that made Johnson and my father sock and sigh, but I never minded, even though I pretended I did in order to keep rank with them. With four-tined forks my father and I pried up the manure in heavy flat cakes gleaming with straw and dropped them into the wheelbarrow. Then we trundled the barrow over and Johnson forked the manure out through a three-foot square mucking hole into a compost heap we would later spread on the fields. The smell wasn't as bad as they made out. It was rather pleasant, warm and heady like fermenting wine.

But the milking area was smallish and it got close and stuffy in there. I hung my shirt on a peg, but they refused to take theirs off.

"It makes me feel nasty and crawly not to have my shirt on in here," Johnson said.

My father nodded. "Anyway, it's getting cooler," he said.

True. What we could see of the sky through the mucking hole had turned dark, and cool air pushed through the hole like breath from a bellows. The same thought came to us all then and we rushed to the hole to see out.

The light went strange. We looked at one another and our faces were darkened like old varnish. The sky turned green and then electric yellow, and a vast blue-black scarp of cloud veered overhead.

"Oh Lord," my father said, and we knew what he meant. An unseasonable storm would probably mean hail, and now with the corn knee-high tender and the tobacco grown too big to reset, we were looking at grim possibilities. "Oh Lord," he said again.

There were curt dim semaphore messages of lightning in the west, south horizon replying to north horizon. We heard the muted trample of thunder. The edges of cloud-scarp mingled green and purple. The intermittent silences were prickly with anticipation; we felt air rush in

69

and out, warm and cool by turns. Then in the west the silver drumming of far rain, west-driven rain coming our way certain.

"I hoped it wouldn't be but I guess it's going to be," Johnson said.

My father said, "Oh Lord."

I had been reading lately a library book of Norse mythology and I thought of Thor. There was a wonderful wild picture of Thor hard at work, his hammer raised above his head, his legs spread heroically apart. His legs reminded me of his name, short and thick and powerful.

We couldn't stop looking, peering bright eyed like squirrels out of a knothole. We thought of the corn and tobacco in worthless ruin, green ribbon on the ground. Only the fragment of a sentence Johnson uttered— "Wouldn't be worth the cutting"—but I knew his whole thought. My father opened his mouth to speak but said nothing.

So then the V-shaped cloud ripped open like a slit featherbed. Cataracts of blue lightning fought against one another, a tangle of unleashed element. Then this uproar ceased for a moment, and we could see above the clouds into the apocalyptic gut of heaven. The harmonious naked thighs of forces, the ruinous concert of airbrawl and fire-shear, and above all this the tender upper reaches of pearl-blue cloud like big empty hospital rooms.

And now the cloud-halves rolled together like elevator doors; and there was a fragrant hollow SHUDder of thunder I felt in my body from crotch to cowlick.

Our hair stood out like spruce needles. We had witnessed the beginning of the storm and couldn't stop looking out at it.

We couldn't stop looking.

The rain was over us now and smells became more vivid, the smell of caked manure and musty straw, the smell even of the wood of the narrow stalls. The first hard lashing of rain on the west wall trembled the barn, tugged the structure at its roots, so that it seemed to try to reach to the bright lightning that poured sidewise across the sky like a bucketful of whitewash tipped over. The thunder gouged out big caverns of ozone.

"Rain, who cares?" my father said. "If only it wouldn't hail."

Johnson said it was coming. "There ain't no way this ain't a storm for hail. It all depends how long it lasts."

We looked into the fields below, flailing gray and silver in gray rain, and we felt as helpless as if we stood by a friend's deathbed. We felt embarrassed, as if we'd promised each other something and had found out we couldn't deliver. We felt slow-witted.

The storm broke a window inside itself and flung the hail in. The stones were at first the size of plums, and I thought they must be hammering big dents in the tin roof.

"Great God Almighty," my father said, and Johnson said, "Yes, you got it right."

The hailstones became smaller and hopped on the ground like tinfoil crickets.

"Maybe the hail is passing a little," my father said. "Maybe we won't be ruined too bad."

"Who can say what will happen?" Johnson's voice sounded so odd that we stared at him and saw him possessed. His red face seemed to glow like an overfired wood heater and his blue eyes lightened almost to white and were as alert as a bobcat's. We shivered to look at him and shivered again with each scattershot of hail that hit the barn wall.

What had happened to Johnson? He was some part of the storm now, or a further element the storm was trying to become, an extension of itself both human and inhuman. Johnson was another kind of presence than a man and we looked away from him, looked out the mucking hole to where a tower of lightning stood.

It was a broad round shaft like a great radiant auger, boring into cloud and mud at once. Burning. Transparent. And inside this cylinder of white-purple light swam shoals of creatures we could never have imagined. Shapes filmy and iridescent and veined like dragonfly wings erranded between the earth and heavens. They were moving to a music we couldn't hear, the thunder blotting it out for us. Or maybe the cannonade of thunder was music for them, but measure that we couldn't understand.

We didn't know what they were.

They were storm angels. Or maybe they were natural creatures whose natural element was storm, as the sea is natural to the squid and shark. We couldn't make out their whole shapes. Were they mermaids or tigers? Were they clothed in shining linen or in flashing armor? We saw what we thought we saw, whatever they were, whatever they were in process of becoming.

This tower of energies went away then, and there was another thrust of lightning just outside the wall. It was a less impressive display, just an ordinary lightning stroke, but it lifted the three of us thrashing in midair for a long moment, then dropped us breathless and sightless on the damp ground. We crawled toward one another and clung together like men overboard in heavy seas. We were bewildered and frightened not by the nearness of death but by the nearness of life; we were buffeted by recognition. Things seemed more completely themselves now, singed with vividness.

We looked at one another dazed, but coming back slowly to everyday reality. We already realized, I think, that our hardest job would be not to talk about what had happened to us, to lessen it and cheapen it with clumsy words. We would have to find some way around it. For a space of time we had become men transfigured, and you don't talk about that. At least, you try not to.

So it was two weeks before I broached the subject to Johnson, one night as we lay in our separate beds in the dark bedroom. "Say, Johnson, you remember that storm and what all went on?"

"Sure, I remember. How'm I going to forget that? We're just lucky it didn't ruin the whole crop and put us plumb out of business."

"Well, right during the awfullest part of it, did you hear a Voice talking? I don't mean one of us, but another Voice?"

He waited a long reluctant time to reply. "What you mean?"

"It seemed to me like I heard a Voice," I declared. "Seemed like it was inside of my head and not inside neither. Only I couldn't understand what it was saying. Did you hear anything like that?"

The darkness between us grew thicker. His breathing slowed and roughened to a soft snore, but I could tell he was pretending.

I didn't mention it to my father until well into autumn. We were trying to find shelter from a slow misty rain. The rain was hardly audible on the leaves overhead, but large drops gathered shiny on the bottoms of the streaky apples hanging about like little Chinese lanterns.

"What kind of voice are you talking about?" he asked, and added: "I wouldn't tell Grandmother about it if I were you."

"Kind of in my head and kind of not," I said. "A big Voice, real big."

"What did It say?"

"I don't know. Some word maybe I don't know. Kind of like *Tet*, and something after that. *Tet* something, maybe. . . I don't know."

He gave me an odd look. "Tet something?"

"Yeah, something. Did you hear a voice during that storm?"

He stared out into the wet air, as if faces he knew would take shape there. At last he nodded, slowly and gravely.

I was excited. "You did? I'm glad to know about it. I was afraid it was just me hearing things."

"I suppose that any storm has got a Voice in it if we took pains to listen," he said.

I wasn't to be distracted. "What did you hear?" I asked. "What did the Voice say to you?"

With his broad hard palm he wiped a raindrop off the end of his nose. "The Voice told me I was right the first time," he said. "That guy Canary is a worthless no-account son of a bitch."

Five / *The Furlough*

Johnson Gibbs, they told me, was coming home from the army.

"It's about time," I said. "I bet he's getting good and tired of that army. I bet he'll be glad to see something good to eat." I was parroting sentences I'd heard around the house for the last six months.

"He won't be here long," my father said. "Just a little while. Then he has to go back."

"Why does he want to go back?"

"He don't want to, he *has* to. That's the way the army is."

"Why is it like that? He ought to come home when he wants to."

"You can't run the army that way," my father said. "Besides, he's not even out of the United States yet. Now he's finished training, they'll send him over to Europe to kill Hitler so we can all be done with this mess."

I wasn't too sure I wanted Johnson to kill Hitler. I'd had a dream, or maybe a waking vision, in which Hitler came upstairs into my room and sat down in Johnson's chair and took off his blood-red riding boots and wiggled his toes in his black socks. When I asked him why he wanted to start wars and kill people, he said, *I'm sorry,*

Jess, but I'm awful tired right now. He did look tired, and his moustache didn't look like the one in the newspaper photographs, but like my Uncle Luden's, a big bushy one all gnawed and ragged at the edges. Then Hitler rose wearily from the chair and crossed over to sit on the edge of Johnson's bed. *If you'll please excuse me, I believe I'll just rest my eyes,* Hitler said, and when he lay back he occupied the exact same space that Johnson did when he slept there. I looked at Hitler and I didn't hate him the way I was supposed to. He just looked tired and silly, and it was obvious that he was no match for Johnson Gibbs. Hitler's hash was settled, the first time he and Johnson ever came together.

"Then what will happen?" I asked.

"Why, then the war will be over and Johnson can come home for good and we'll get this farm in shape and I'll get us a new baseball and some new gloves. I'll get you a new glove too."

"When is he coming to see us just-to-visit?"

"In a few days."

Johnson didn't show up during the day, however. He arrived sometime during the night while I was sleeping, and when I woke in the morning I saw him in the big bed across from me. It was all I could do to hold myself back from shouting and leaping on his bed, but I waited a moment and had cooler thoughts.

I tiptoed over and looked down at the sleeping soldier. That's how I thought of him, not as Johnson Gibbs but as "the sleeping soldier"; and I was certain that the army had changed him in important ways, though I couldn't tell how. He looked the same to me; perhaps his hair was a little blonder. He lay on his side with his back toward me, breathing deeply. I stepped forward to touch his hair, but my bare foot hurt where I brought it down on the sharp corner of a brick. There were two bricks and a large rock on the floor, and I remembered that this was the play-pretend land mine that I had put in Johnson's bed and covered with the blanket so that if any Germans came through the window and over Johnson's bed they would have been blown to bits. Now I reflected that if my mine had killed anybody it would have been Johnson and I felt obscurely ashamed and a little scared.

His khaki uniform lay folded precisely on the chair and I went over and examined it for a long time, running my finger along the crisply starched folds and touching the gleaming buttons and the shiny friction belt buckle. I wanted to see Johnson in his uniform as soon as possible because it would be the uniform that made him a different person, that turned him into the man who was going to kill Hitler.

I went back to my bed, unhooked my milking clothes from the bedpost, and ran downstairs. My father was waiting for me on the side porch, smoking his cigarette in the cold November dawn. "Johnson is here," I said. "He must've come in last night while we were asleep."

"While *you* were asleep," he said. "We got up and let him in and welcomed him."

"Why didn't you wake me up?"

"Because you're a growing boy and you need your beauty rest. You better get all you can, since it looks to me like you're going to grow up to be mighty ugly."

"You could've got me up. I ain't no little boy no more."

"Maybe," he said. His honey-colored hair was un-combed and his eyes were red rimmed. "Maybe you're not and maybe you are. You're big enough to wear shoes in November, ain't you?"

I had forgotten to put my shoes on, and as soon as he mentioned it, my feet felt freezing. I sneaked back up into the room and got my shoes and socks. Johnson hadn't stirred. I brought them back down to the porch to put on.

"Hurry up, Jess," my father said. "We're running late this morning."

"I'll be glad for breakfast time," I said. "I want to hear Johnson tell us all about it."

Then we went on to the barn and milked the four cows and let them out into the pasture and came back to the house and poured the milk into the big steel cans and set them out for the dairy to pick up. It seemed to take twice as long as usual to get the work done, and in my excitement I kept fumbling things so that it seemed to take three times as long. But finally we went in through the warm steamy kitchen for breakfast.

Johnson wasn't there.

"He's overslept," I said. "I better go and get him up."

"Jess," my mother said, "if you wake Johnson up, I'll—I'll . . . I don't know what I'll do."

"Jerk a knot in his frame," my father suggested. "Nail his hide to the barn door. Pop his eyes out of his head and gobble them down like raisins."

"Something like that," she promised gravely.

"Well, what am I going to do?" I cried.

"You're going to school, the same as usual," she said. "You can see Johnson when you get back this afternoon."

"Oh no," I said. The school day appeared before me in all its gruesome length, the most glacially slow day ever recorded on any calendar.

"Don't worry," she said. "You'll get to spend plenty of time with our soldier-boy."

But no.

When I got home at 3:30 and flung down my satchel and weary school books, I was told by my grandmother that Johnson had gone off after lunch and wasn't expected back until suppertime, at least. "Aw no," I said. "Where'd he go?"

"I believe he's got a little personal business to attend to," she said.

"What kind of business? He could've took me to help him out, if he's got something to do."

"This is kind of a one-man job," she said. "I believe he's took to sparking that Laurie Lee that lives up on Youngson Hill. There's not much way you could help him with that."

"A *girl*?"

"A right pretty girl, is what I hear tell." She grinned.

I was thunderstruck. Johnson had never said anything good about girls that I could remember. Once he had told me all the things that girls couldn't do: fly fish, play football, fix car motors, or climb trees. It seemed to me they could climb trees all right if they would just concentrate and practice up some, but he said they couldn't do it because they wore dresses and if they got up in a tree they'd show their fannies and that was a shame on a girl.

"What about those girls showing their fannies in Uncle Luden's peepshow?" I asked. "They ain't got a stitch on."

"Well, that's a different sort of girl," he said. "They're from California."

"Do girls show their fannies in California?"

"I certainly do hope so," he said, "and I certainly hope to find out."

But Laurie Lee was no California girl; she was old man McClain Lee's oldest daughter and she liked to dress up in her yellow dress and go to see Lana Turner or John Garfield in the movies. I'd sat beside her at a Garfield movie one time, and she was so redolent of a sweet perfume that I got a headache. She wore her dark black hair in the glamour-girl style and must have spent hours getting the coiffure right. Sometimes I would see her in Sherman's drugstore, sitting at a table with a dish of ice cream and leafing through a movie magazine.

So I knew who she was, all right, but I thought that she didn't know me, being interested only in older boys with cars and argyle sweaters. That was fine because all she cared about was a bunch of mushy silliness, lovestuff and all that. Nothing about her to attract Johnson Gibbs. But I had been wrong about Johnson, and I knew that it was the army that had changed him. It was probably because he had to eat such horrible food in the army that he had taken up with Laurie Lee. Seemed to me that the army wasn't doing anything right; it had already drafted thousands of men and none of them had killed Hitler yet, so now they were having to send Johnson to do it, but he was already distracted by a girl and would probably forget what he was supposed to be up to. It came to me that Laurie Lee was a Nazi spy, and her mission was to confuse Johnson and find out his secret plan. She was probably writing down everything he told her, and when he left she went to her hidden apparatus and sent a message in Morse code to Hitler.

She didn't much look like a Nazi spy when Johnson brought her home for supper. They sat out on the side porch, waiting for the meal with my father, and she and Johnson chewed gum at breakneck speed.

Johnson grinned when he saw me and his big face grew red and happy. "Hello there, General, where you been?"

He'd never called me General before, and I wasn't sure how I liked it. "I been right here," I said. "Where *you* been?"

"Oh, round and about . . . You know Jess, don't you, Laurie?"

"Of course I do," she said. "Hello there, Sweet Thing."

When she called me Sweet Thing, I felt a bit relieved because it was clear she was too dumb to be a Nazi spy. Hitler was too smart and mean to put up with somebody who said such truck as that, and I began to wonder if Johnson was really as bright as I'd always thought he was.

I said Hello to her, feeling uncomfortable. Then I asked Johnson, "How come you didn't wake me up when you came in last night?"

"I was mighty tired," he said, "and a fellow needs to be fresh and alert when he meets up with you. I was so tired I could almost have slept on rocks and bricks. Not quite, but almost." He winked at me.

I could see that he had changed. He was an older person than he used to be; he'd had to make himself older because of the war. And I felt that I should go about getting older too; it was my responsibility. The first thing I would do would be to pack up all my toys and put them away. No more play-pretend, either, with rocks and bricks and so forth. All that was behind me now, and I straightened my shoulders back and began to talk like an adult.

"Have you seen any Germans yet?"

"Not where I've been," he said. "But they told us what they looked like."

"What like?"

"Terrible," he said. "Ugliest-looking things you ever thought of. Makes you shiver to think about them."

"Have you shot an army rifle yet?"

"Sure, lots of times. Nothing to it. I'll show you my marksman's medal after a while."

So that was all right, then. He hadn't clean forgotten what they were sending him to do; he was practicing.

"What grade are you in now, Jess?" Laurie asked me.

"Third."

"How do you like it?"

"It's okay," I said. "I'd rather be in the army, though."

"I know what you mean," she said. "There's something about a soldier." She squeezed Johnson's arm and his face turned a brilliant scarlet. He murmured something to her and she took her hands off him, but she wasn't displeased and looked across at my father and winked.

He smiled at her but didn't wink back.

I didn't get to talk to Johnson that night either. After supper he and Laurie Lee sat at the table and talked with us a few minutes and then they went off together. Johnson borrowed our old Pontiac and Laurie nestled as close to him in the front seat as she could. They drove off slowly, waving back at us.

"They're mighty tight together," my father said. "I don't believe you could slip a dollar bill edgeways between them."

"Where are they going?" I asked.

"Jess honey," my mother said, "it's been so long that I've forgotten. You'll have to ask your father."

"Where?" I said.

"I believe they're headed up the Primrose Path to Sweet Perdition," he said. "With maybe a stop off at Flagrante Delicto."

"I never heard of those places. How do you get there?"

"If Johnson's got any sense, they'll go by way of Rubber Junction," he answered.

"Joe Robert. . ." That was my mother's warning tone of voice, and it meant that my father had to begin talking about something else. That suited me because I didn't understand what he was talking about in the first place.

"Can I stay up till Johnson gets back and talk to him?"

"Not tonight," my mother said. "He'll be back too late. Don't worry, Jess, you'll have plenty of time to be with Johnson." There was a note of deep sadness in her voice when she said his name. I heard it faithfully but didn't understand. There were too many things suddenly that I didn't understand, and I didn't know what to do about it. I knew that I needed to be older, and I was trying to will myself to be older, but that's not enough. You have to have some basic information that was not yet available to me.

I did get to talk to Johnson that night, though. I didn't know when he came in, but when I woke up in the deep morning he was sitting on the edge of his bed with his hands open in his lap, staring at nothing, at the gray-yellow shadow that the lamp on the big black table between us cast under the chair. His face looked so still and melancholy that I didn't want to speak at first, and merely lay with my head propped on my arm and watched him. I knew he was aware that I was awake, but for a long time he didn't speak either.

Then he said softly, "I don't want to go back, Jess, and I ain't sure I'm going to."

"You're not going back to the army?"

It took him a long time to turn his head to look at me. "The army ain't like you imagine. It's a lot different from what you think."

"Where will you go?"

"Thinking I might go AWOL."

"What's that?"

"A.W.O.L.," he said. "Absent With Ole Laurie."

"Is that okay to do?"

"No. I'd be in a pile of trouble. But I'm thinking about it anyhow."

"Why don't you just quit? Tell the army you don't want to work there no more."

"You can't quit the army," he said. "They lock you up and burn the key. Or they take and shoot you."

That one was almost too much for me, but it fitted right in with what I knew about the army not doing anything right. Here was Johnson Gibbs, who was their best chance to kill Hitler, and they were going to shoot him.

"It would've been all right if I hadn't lived here," he said. "The army would have been a good place for me, lot better than what I was used to. But then I came here and got to know you-all folks, part of the family and all, and as soon as I got used to it I had to leave. And the army don't treat a man like you folks do."

"It's funny you wanting to get out," I said, "because my father wants to get in."

"They won't take him," Johnson said. "He's the sole support of this family; he's got to keep this farm going. That's plenty enough job."

"After you kill Hitler, you'll come back and help us farm."

"I don't know as I'm the man to kill Hitler," he said. "Like as not, he's the man to kill me."

"Nah," I said, "that's plumb silly. You're just talking foolishness now."

He smiled a dim far-off unhappy smile. "Probably you're right, Jess. Maybe I'd better have a little talk with your father before I do something pretty dumb. . . . What say we get us some sleep now?"

During the next few days there was a nervousness in the house. My father and mother and grandmother went about with worried expressions, and they gathered in set-apart places to confer with one another in low tones. I knew what they were talking about, so it didn't bother me, except that I wished they'd ask for my opinion. I thought that Johnson ought to return to the army right now and go on to Europe and complete his mission. Then the army would be finished with him and he could come back to the farm. As soon as he was out of the army, he would change back to the way he used to be, and he wouldn't think twice about Laurie Lee or any other girl.

But they never asked for my opinion. Instead, my father asked old man McClain Lee to the house and sat him down, gave him a cup of coffee, and inquired if he'd heard about any plans that Laurie and Johnson had made.

"If they got plans, they ain't told me," he said. He was a weary-looking little man with gray hair and gray eyes and discolored teeth. He had six children, three girls and three boys, and I'd heard my father say that it must be a pretty tough go for old man Lee. His wife had been dead for ten years and his mother moved in to help do for them. But she too had died in a short while and his maiden sister, who was not entirely right in the head, had taken her mother's place. He seemed shrunken in his clothes, and there was something furtive about him; he cast his eyes sidelong like a dog wary of kicks.

"Well, McClain," my father said, "you know I'm not one to carry tales. . ." He had drawn up a chair close to Mr. Lee's, so that their knees were almost touching, and now he paused for confirmation of his remark.

The old man gave him a curious glance and a slow nod.

" . . . And Lord knows I'm not one to stand in the way of good ole True Love, but we've got reason to think that our lad, Johnson, and your Laurie are maybe planning on running off to get married."

Mr. Lee's left eyebrow twitched once. "Have you heard them say so?" He took a slow noisy sip of coffee.

"Not in so many words," my father said. "But I've got to where I know Johnson pretty well, and just putting together some little comments he's made here and there, I think maybe that's what's in the wind."

The old man thought for a while. "Well, I don't know as I could stop them if I wanted to. They appear both to be about full growed, and that Laurie, whatever I tell her, she does just the other thing."

"Now, McClain, you don't mean to say you'd look with favor on this match-up. My thought is, it would be an awful mistake."

"It's theirn to make, though, ain't it?" He gave my father a level look.

"Sure enough," he said, "but they've got the good Lord's plenty of time to make it in. I just don't believe this is the best time, all in a rush. I say, let them wait a while, see how they feel maybe in a year or so. You know Johnson doesn't have prospect one, McClain, an orphan boy in the army without a scrap of money to his name."

"He's got his army pay," Mr. Lee said. "I know them that's started with less."

From his tone of voice I knew he meant that he had started with less. I tried to picture Johnson a long time from now as Mr. Lee, gray and small and weary, but I couldn't do it. Not the army and not even marrying a girl could cause that much change in him.

"McClain, the point is that these furlough marriages usually don't work out," my father said. "Just as soon as they're hitched they'll be separated no telling how long. Johnson will be overseas, like as not, and Laurie will be back here married, counting the days. You know there ain't no hope in that situation."

"I wouldn't know how to stop them, even if I wanted to," Mr. Lee said. He set his half-finished cup of pale coffee on the floor and stood up. "What you're saying is true, I reckon, the best way you see it. But I've seen couples I didn't think had a flea's chance do right well."

"You're not interested in discouraging them even a little bit?"

"Sure thing. When I hear about it, I'll act like I'm plumb tickled pink. If that don't make Laurie back up, I don't know what will."

My father sighed. "Well, maybe that's the best we can do." We walked out with Mr. Lee, who now began talking about the miserable weather, the terrible outlook for crops this year, and the rotten state of politics. My father agreed with him, making soothing noises. But when he came back into the room, he was muttering "Dumb son of a bitch" under his breath. Then he sighed again and said aloud, "Well, maybe you can't blame him too much for wanting one less mouth to feed. It's a pretty tough go for the old man."

"Is Johnson going to marry Laurie Lee?" I asked.

"No," my father said.

"How do you know?"

"I'm going to stop him."

"How?"

He rubbed his earlobe. "That's the part I don't know yet."

Next day he said, "What I want you to do, Jess, is steal all of Johnson's chewing gum and bring it to me."

That was easy enough to do. Johnson and Laurie Lee had been out until late into the night and Johnson was sleeping in this Saturday morning. I made my way over to his bed and watched. His mouth was open and his eyes rolled wildly under the closed lids; his left hand clasped and unclasped. I knew that he was having a bad dream and at another time I might have awakened him, but now I was confused about what kind of relationship we had. I wasn't sure how he'd take me.

There were four packages of gum on the big table at the foot of the bed, mixed in with pocket change, and another package in his shirt pocket. Four of these were open, a stick or two missing from each. I took them downstairs and out onto the side porch. "Here they are," I told my father.

"Mostly broken packs," he said. "That's good." He began taking the sticks out and unwrapping them carefully, slipping down the yellow Beechnut sleeves and laying them to one side. Then he took six packages of another kind of gum out of the pocket of his plaid wool jacket and began doing the same thing. The gum he had brought was in dark purple wrappers, but I couldn't see what kind it was. He slid the new gum into the yellow sleeves and put them back into the packages. When he came to the unopened package of Beechnut he paused, then muttered, "He won't notice one more broken pack," and zipped it open and performed the same operation.

Then he lit a cigarette and surveyed his work. "That ought to do," he said. "Can't see a bit of difference."

"What is it?" I asked. "How's different chewing gum going to make any difference?"

"I'll miss my guess if it doesn't cool his ardor considerable. Anyhow, it'll spoil his concentration. Now, Jess, I don't want you to be chewing any of Johnson's gum, no matter how many times he offers it. You understand?"

"Yes sir."

He gathered up the foiled sticks of Beechnut and the purple wrappers of the new gum and held them out to me. "Here, take all this stuff and bury it in a hole behind the woodshed. Then take these others back up to Johnson's room and put them back exactly the way you found them. Can you do that?"

"Yes sir." I took the handful of gum and paper. Behind the woodshed I smoothed out one of the purple wrappers and read it. *Feenamint.* I'd never heard of it.

But it changed Johnson's behavior in notable ways. He began to spend what seemed hours in the downstairs bathroom, and an equal number of hours in the little one upstairs. He would be sitting at his ease, talking, out on the porch or at the dinner table, when suddenly he would stand up and say, "Excuse me," in a tiny pinched voice and rush away. Then we'd hear the bathroom door open and slam shut with a loud bang. Over the next few days this happened scores of times.

My grandmother and mother began to exchange puzzled glances. "I believe something's wrong with Johnson," my mother said. "Something with his health."

"Diet," my father said. "He's been eating that factory-made army food, and now he comes home to this good country cooking. Shock like that, bound to mess up a fellow's innards."

"It didn't seem to bother him at first," she said.

"I don't think it's anything serious," he said. "I wouldn't worry about it."

It became even more awkward when Laurie Lee came over to visit because she did exactly the same thing Johnson did. She would be sitting talking nice as pie and empty as wind about one of her favorite movie stars, then stand up red faced and tear off to the bathroom, slamming the door. She'd been chewing Johnson's gum, I knew.

"I may need to work on that bathroom door," my father said. "Sounds like it's getting a little loose on its hinges. That's if I can find a time somebody ain't using it."

There was one awful instance when Laurie sped to the bathroom only to find that Johnson already occupied it. We heard her knock on the door, then begin banging on it. "Hurry up, Johnson," she cried. "*Please!*"

"I believe this romance might be simmering down a little," my father said. "You notice she didn't call him Honey-dear and Sweetie-pie, for a blessed change."

"There must be something wrong with the kids," my mother said. "I think they've caught some kind of germ."

"Nah-nah," he said. "They're just all flustered and excited. That's Young Romance for you, Cora. You've just forgot."

"That's not the way it affected *me*," she said.

"Ah well," he said, "love is a great mystery, you know. Hits some folks one way and some another. Capricious. Liable to come and go like a summer shower."

"I'm beginning to think you have something to do with this, Joe Robert."

"Me?" my father said. He stared at her, innocent as a cow.

We head Laurie Lee say, "Johnson, please please please *please* hurry up!" It was the wail of a lost soul condemned to eternal darkness and sorrow.

Came a night when Johnson didn't go out on a date with Laurie Lee, but stayed home with us. He had only five days left of his furlough, and we all felt sympathy for him. His face was no longer its customary fiery red color, but paler, almost white in patches. We ate a leisurely supper and then moved into the other room to enjoy the heat of the cast-iron stove. We talked in ordinary fashion about old times, the good times we'd all had together before Johnson went into the army, and no one took any notice of Johnson springing up to run to the bathroom every little while. At one point the talk turned to the war in Europe and the probable plans of the Allies, but my mother veered us away from that subject.

"I just can't bear to think about that with Johnson having to go back," she said. There was a bright wetness in her eyes, tears that didn't form into teardrops.

"I don't like to think about it either," Johnson said over his shoulder, on his way to the bathroom.

My father began talking about a fishing trip that he and Johnson had taken. They'd gone to Fontana Lake to try their luck, and he told about the crazy old man they'd rented a boat from, about falling asleep in the boat with their lines out and having to row back a quarter of a mile to disengage their hooks, and about the single fish they had caught. "Some kind of catfish," he said, "but it was a breed of catfish I never heard of. I swear that was the ugliest fish I ever saw. Johnson and me both couldn't stand to look at it, much less bring it back and admit we'd been associating with it. What'd we ever do with that ugly thing, Johnson?"

Johnson started to laugh, then said, "Excuse me," in that squeaky little voice and rushed away. We heard the bathroom door.

My father grinned. "Now I recall," he said. "We buried it up on a sandbank. Dug a trench and put up a little old wood-cross grave marker. Johnson scratched an epitaph for it there in the sand. *Too ugly to look at, Too ugly to eat, The son of a bitch took all our bait.*"

"The time I remember best was the picnic on Betsey's Gap," my mother said. "You remember when you boys wanted to bring me that wild flower you saw growing on the cliff face?"

"Big blue jack-in-the-pulpit," my father said. "I believe that was about the prettiest flower ever I saw. But it was a trial climbing up to it."

"I think it must have been," she said. "There wasn't much left of it by the time you got it down to me. All smashed into pulp."

"Well, getting up wasn't half as hard as getting down," my father said. "There was no way down off of there but just to fall. I'd fall a piece, and while I was hurtling by Johnson I'd pass the flower off to him. Like a football. Then when he was falling down past me, he'd hand it off. Finally one of us fell on the flower and squashed it good. Was that you or me fell on it, Johnson?"

"I think—" Johnson began, but suddenly grinned a white tight grin and gritted out, "Excuse me," and cleared off toward the bathroom.

"I believe I was the one smushed it," my father said. "Pitifulest-looking excuse for a flower. I wanted to bury it like with the fish. But Johnson said to bring it to you, it's the thought that counts."

"I really am worried about his health," my mother said. "I'm thinking about calling the doctor."

"Don't do it, Cora," he said. "You got to trust me he'll be all right."

She looked at him then and we knew that she knew something, but she didn't know what.

We sat and talked a while longer and then went off to bed. Johnson and I climbed up the spooky stairs to our room. We got undressed and into bed and lay there a few minutes, thinking about the good time we'd had just jawing around the stove.

He sighed heavily in the dark. "That's the kind of thing I've missed so awful much," he said. "I reckon I'll miss it all the more when I go back."

"Are you going back?" I asked. "You're not going to run away with Laurie Lee?"

For a while he didn't answer. Then he said, "It ain't worked out too well for us, Jess. We can't even look at each other without having to wind-sprint to the shithouse."

I remembered my father's phrase. "But what if it's good ole True Love?"

"I think it must not be. Not in any way I ever heard tell of, anyhow."

"I wonder what it's like," I said. "Real True Love, I mean."

He sighed again. "I don't know. But it ought to be a damn sight more interesting disease than diarrhea."

Then we fell asleep.

The next Saturday morning his furlough was over. It was planned for us all to ride with him over to the Tipton train station and see him off. But one after another we hung back and said we couldn't go, that there was some task or other needing urgent attention. The truth was that we couldn't bear to see him get on the train, lost in a crowd of soldiers and strangers; we couldn't bear to watch the train pull out of the dumpy little station, its black engine smoke like a pall, and hear the weeping of the kinfolk of soldiers far and near.

At last neither my mother or father would drive him to the station and they had a few words about it. But it was no angry argument between them because they knew that the cause was their mutual sorrow, and finally my father gave in.

Johnson came downstairs in his army uniform, and though it was the first time I'd seen him wear it, he didn't look strange to me. He looked like he belonged in it; it was as natural to him as his red complexion, which was returning to its usual state now that my father and I had got rid of the Feenamint and restored Johnson to a diet of Beechnut. He wore a solemn, but not glum, expression, and his jawline was hard; he was clenching his teeth.

There was a tearful round of hugging and handshakes. My grandmother gave him a little red New Testament, my mother a box of fried chicken and cookies, and my father pressed some money into his hand.

But no one said anything. What could we say? The world outside our hills had come over the mountaintops like a great black cloud full of lightning and thunder, full of shattering voices which were alien to us, voices speaking in languages we had never truly believed to exist. And this cloud of voices muttered of the destruction of cultures and civilizations to which we hardly belonged, to which we had only the most tenuous of allegiances, yet to which we were paying the most precious of tributes.

I had learned now from hearing my parents and Johnson talk that Johnson was not really going to kill Hitler and end the war, that nothing was to be that simple, that the terror-striking cloud which darkened our mountains would dissipate only by force of natural time and process, and that Johnson was but a smallest part of this stormy process, a fragile walnut leaf blown about in an eruption of gale. I had learned, maybe without really knowing, that not even the steadfast mountains themselves were safe and unmoving, that the foundations of the earth were shaken and the connections between the stars become frail as cobweb.

I believe that all of us felt these thoughts just now at the moment of Johnson's departure, and our thoughts were so awesome to us that no one could speak a word, not even *good-bye*. We hugged and clasped and wept silently.

Even after my father drove Johnson away my grandmother and mother and I said nothing, but went up on the porch to wait in the cold wind for my father to return. Perhaps we would never speak again; perhaps, without meaning to, we had taken a religious vow we could not understand.

But when he returned from the train station my father was smiling and joking, and we began to feel not quite so sad.

"I think I've figured out why I'm so crazy about ole Johnson," he said. "It's because he thinks exactly like I do. He even talks like me, a little bit."

"Now I wonder why that is," my mother said.

The Telegram

*The telegram was always there, not to be got rid of. It
was never opened; we knew what was in it. The telegram told us that Johnson Gibbs was dead, that he had
been killed in a training accident at Fort Bragg. A mor-
tar round had exploded where and when it had no business to. Others were injured, only Johnson was killed,
just a few days before he was to be shipped overseas.*

*There was an outburst of weeping at first, especially
my mother wept, but later there was no more. A flinty
silence descended upon the house, there was a hard gray
feeling in us. Inside my throat it was hard as steel; I
thought that if I rapped my chest with my knuckles it
would ring like a suit of armor. We wandered about
dazed and mechanical.*

*For a long time the telegram sat on the dining table,
propped against the blue-and-white ringed sugar bowl.
The telegram glowed yellow like an ugly pus, and no
one would touch it. Neither could we bear to see it there,
and we took two weeks of meals out on the porch.*

*Then someone—my father, it must have been—re-
moved it but it came back. Everyone took it away, but it
always returned to its place on the table, propped there
to stare at us.*

I found a proper hiding place for it, a rat hole out in the woodshed. It felt hot in my hands when I carried it, not like paper at all but like a burning slime. I stuffed it into the hole and sealed the hole with a rock. There were red and white burn streaks on my hand where I had carried the telegram and I had to wash my hands a long time before they went away.

Then that evening at sundown it was back on the table, leaning there against the sugar bowl. It was still unwrinkled, as pristine as when it had first been delivered.

But none of us could remember its being delivered.

Once I saw my mother bearing away a wooden tray heaped over with dish towels and I knew that underneath the towels lay the telegram and that she had formed a plan to get rid of it. I admired her bravery, but I thought that her plan—whatever it was—wouldn't work, and it didn't. The telegram reappeared, insolent and undamaged.

It was on the table there and none of us would so much as glance at it. But of course we kept gazing at it as if it were the only light on in the darkest night of the world.

My father took it to the top of a pasture hill and laid it in the grass and set fire to it with a kitchen match. It curled in slow agony and burned away smokeless, leaving an oblong of yellow sear that would never grow green again. By the time he got back to the house it was waiting for him on the red tablecloth.

At night it crept over our sleep like a great sheet of yellow ice, and we felt it was suffocating us in our beds and sat up dry-eyed but drenched with sweat.

One time this yellow ice came during the day, an endless glacier. We struggled upon it against the desperate winds and the sky's moaning. We held hands and guarded our faces against the wind and against each other's gaze and it was a long time before we made it back to the farm, to the house among the warm hills and fields.

The telegram had the power of becoming smaller, shrinking to the size of a postage stamp or to a mere speck, a mote. Then I would find it in my pocket or in the bedclothes. Often it seemed to have lodged in the corner of my eye, a yellow spot that would not go away and caused my eye to burn and water. That was the worst physical pain, when we couldn't wash it out of our eyes even with weeping.

Yet in all these weeks we never talked about it, never mentioned it at all. That seemed strange to me, that the telegram brought us so much pain and fear and we wouldn't speak of it. Perhaps we were afraid that if we talked about it, it would grow more omnipresent and we would never escape its power.

I prayed that it would be removed from us. I have never prayed so earnestly since, with such guileless passion. I knew that all of us were praying, my grandmother continuously night and day. But the prayers had no effect on the telegram, and seemed not even to alleviate the dead feeling in our hearts. It was then I found out that I could pray in despair and the despair might only deepen, that I could form the words and cling to the meaning of them even though my spirit had shriveled within me to a pinpoint.

Then one evening I pulled a chair to the table and sat down to stare at the telegram. Let it do to me what it can, I thought. It was just at dusk and the telegram was the brightest object in the room. I don't know how long I sat looking. The room darkened and stars appeared in the upper windowpanes. At last the telegram began to change shape. Slowly wrinkling and furling inward, it took the form of a yellow rose, hand-sized, with layer on layer of glowing yellow petals. It seemed to hover an inch or so above the tablecloth. It uttered a mournful little whimper then, a sound I had once heard a blind puppy make when it could not find its mother's warm flank. And with that sound it disappeared from my sight forever, tumbled spiraling down a hole in the darkness. I watched it go away and my heart lightened then and I was able to rise, shaken and confused, and walk from the room without shame, not looking back, finding my way confidently in the dark.

I think that my grandmother and mother and father each had to undergo this ritual, and I think that we each saw the telegram take a different transformation before it disappeared, but we never spoke of that either.

It was an agonizing rite to undergo, hardest of all for my mother.

Six / *The Storytellers*

Uncle Zeno came to visit us. Or did he?

Not even the bare fact of his visit is incontestable. He was a presence, all right; he told stories, endless stories, and these stories worked upon the fabric of our daily lives in such manner that we began to doubt our own outlines. Sometimes, walking in the country, one comes upon an abandoned flower garden overtaken by wild flowers. Is it still a garden? The natural and the artificial orders intermingle, and ready definition is lost.

But the man who effected such transformation seemed hardly to be among us. He was a slight, entirely unremarkable man given to wearing white shirts with frayed cuffs and collars. That is, in fact, how my memory characterizes him: a frayed cuff, a shred, a nibbled husk. If he had not spoken we might have taken no more notice of him than of one of the stray cats which made our barn a sojourn between wilderness and wilderness. His hair, his face and hands, I cannot recollect. He was a voice.

The voice too was unremarkable, except that it was inexhaustible. Dry, flat, almost without inflection, it delivered those stories with the mechanical precision of an ant toting a bit of leaf mold to its burrow. Yet Uncle

Zeno had no discernible purpose in telling his stories, and there was little arrangement in the telling. He would begin a story at the beginning, in the middle, or at the end; or he would seize upon an odd detail and stretch into his stories in two or three directions at once. He rarely finished a story at one go; he would leave it suspended in midair like a gibbeted thief or let it falter to a halt like a stalled car blocking the road. And he took no interest in our reactions. If the story was funny our laughter made no more impression upon him than a distant butterfly; when we were downcast at a sad story, he did not seem to realize it. His attention was fixed elsewhere. My father and I got the impression that he was not remembering or inventing his stories, but repeating words whispered to him by another voice issuing from somewhere behind the high, fleecy clouds he loved to stare at.

That puts me in mind of . . .

These six flat monosyllables will be spoken at break of Judgment Day; they are the leisurely herald notes which signal that time has stopped, that human activity must suspend and every attention be bent toward discovering the other leisurely country words which follow. This is the power that beginnings have over us; we must find out what comes next and cannot pursue even the most urgent of our personal interests with any feeling of satisfaction until we do find out. The speaker of these words holds easy dominion.

That puts me in mind of—Uncle Zeno said—Lacey Joe Blackman. You know how proud some folks are of what they've got—he said—cars and fine houses and such. Some folks are proud of their wonderful hunting dogs, like Buford Rhodes was, but I ain't talking about him but about Lacey Joe Blackman. Lacey Joe was proud of a watch which come down to him from his daddy and Lacey Joe kept it on him for fifty years or better, and he couldn't say how long it had been in the family before his daddy. It was real old-fashioned, a big fat bib watch in a silver casing and been around so long the silver had wore thin on it like a dime. Even when he got to be seventy-five years old Lacey Joe was liable to tug his watch out and flip up the lid and give you the time of day, you didn't need to ask.

Lacey Joe had a well-known name as a hunter, maybe only Turkey George Palmer had killed more brutes, and Lacey Joe would go on a hunt anytime night or day— deer, bear, groundhog, you name it. Go a-hunting piss-ants I reckon if they was in season. They ain't much bear hunting in these parts any more, I remember the last time Lacey Joe went.

Setback Williams had sold his big farm down on Bea-verdam, as he was getting on in years, and him and Mary Sue had bought a little homestead that butted up against the Smoky National Park. No farming on it, Setback was past doing any heavy labor, but there was a little apple orchard in the back, maybe two dozen trees, and old Set-back liked his apples and his apple trees.

But there was a troublesome bear ranging in those acres and he liked the apples and the apple trees powerful well too. You know how it is with a bear and the apple trees, gets all excited and he'll go to sharpening his claws like a cat with a settee. Go around and around a tree rip-ping at the bark and pretty soon he's girdled it and that tree is doomed to die.

Setback had done already lost two trees to this bear and he didn't know what to do. Can't shoot a bear any-more even if he's on your property unless you get permis-sion from the Park Service and they won't hardly never give permission no matter what cussedness a bear has been up to. But Setback called anyhow over there to the Ranger Station I don't know how many times and kept deviling them and finally they were out to his place and allowed as how maybe he had a problem.

What they done was put up a fence, but the Park Ser-vice won't put you up no barbwire fence because it ain't what they call rustic-like, they don't want no tourist looking at a barbwire fence. They put up a heavy peel-log fence around the orchard about six foot high, ten times as much work as a good barbwire fence, and Setback took one look at it and declared, Boys, that ain't going to keep no bear off of my apple trees. And it wasn't two days later he went out and there was a bear setting in a tree, looking down like he owned that tree and the U.S. Park Service too. Setback raised a holler and the bear scuttled down and lickety-split into the forest right over the fence. Didn't make no more of that fence than you would a plate of peach cobbler.

So he called the Rangers again and they dawdled and cussed awhile and finally come over and built another peel-log fence, never seen anything like it. This one was fourteen foot high if it was an inch and strong as a fort. Kind of awesome to look at, think about the work them fellers had put into it. But Setback wasn't nothing only suspicious, and a week later he looks out and there was that same bear up in that same tree. Like the King of England on his throne all of gold. Setback ran out and hollered and the bear jumped down and run to the fence. When he got there he stretched up like a man reaching down a jug off of a tall shelf and took hold of the middle log about seven foot high and leapt up and then he was over. It was plumb pretty to look at, Setback said, except he was so mad.

He was on the telephone in a jiffy and told them he was going to shoot that bear, National Park or no National Park, and they said No he wasn't. He told them a man has a right to protect his property, especially the apple trees, and also besides his wife was getting scared, that bear coming in on them all the time. That was where he was stretching it because Mary Sue never took fright of nothing, stouthearted she was. Finally they said they'd let him trap the bear as long as he used the trap they'd bring him, and he could hold it and they'd come and pick up the bear and carry it to the farthest-back part of the forest and it wouldn't wander out as far as his apple trees again. He suspicioned that wouldn't work neither, but he was willing to try anything.

The trap they brought him didn't have no teeth,

smoothed off so it wouldn't hurt a bear's leg much, but it was awful big and heavy, Setback said he never seen one that big.

He pegged it in the ground out there amongst the trees. Used a locust stake must have been five foot long and a big old drag chain. Covered it over with leaves all proper.

Might be another week passed before Setback and Mary Sue heard the awfulest row and tearing-around and uproar. It was the early hour of the morning, not what you call sunlight yet. Bothersome to be woke up like that, but when it come to Setback they must have caught the bear he hustled into his clothes and went out to have a look.

But there was nothing to see but some tore-up leaves and rassled-around dirt. Not one other blessed thing. That bear had pulled that five-foot stake plumb out of the ground. Hadn't left nothing, toted off the trap, the drag chain, and the locust stake, and gone over that fourteen-foot log fence. Hard to believe his eyes, Setback said.

He was back on the phone to the Rangers again, telling them what he was going to do and them saying Yessir right along. Because you couldn't leave the animal with the trap on his leg, him in pain like that. Then he called up me and five others and Lacey Joe Blackman who still kept his bear dogs and always had such a name for bear hunting. And we met over at his place it must have been about eight o'clock in the morning.

The dogs got the scent right in a hurry, all barking to beat Joshua, and we set off in a trot. We kept an eye on Lacey Joe, him going on eighty years of age, but he was hale and spry and after a little bit we figured he would wear us down and the dogs too. Didn't have far to go, though, maybe two miles and the bear was already treed.

An awful big tree too, sixty foot tall anyhow, and spindly at the top where he was at. He was right in the very tip-top, and the tree was bowed way over with him. If it wasn't a pine tree you'd think it might bust. And just enough wind to sway it, and the bear in it, that was some sight. We stood just a-looking for a long time.

Till Setback says, Well, Lacey Joe Blackman, I believe it's up to you to take the first shot. Him being the oldest, and us all thinking he was about half sand-blind and one of us would get the kill. I'll do her if that's what you want, he says, and steps out and raises up his rifle. Which we seen was an old thirty-aught-six must've belonged to Nimrod and didn't even have a front sight. We was all thinking, that bear ain't got no worries just yet, and he steps out and raised up his rifle and didn't take no aim and killed that bear stone dead. Bullet we found out later went right between the eyes.

The bear dropped plummet. Down about thirty foot and then jerked up again. That locust stake he'd been dragging got caught crossways in the fork of a big old limb and held him up there. The tree was bending way over. And the bear hung up like that went back and forth like a pend'lum on a grandfather clock. Back and forth, and back and forth. It was a sight made us all stand there quiet as pallbearers.

And so Lacey Joe Blackman, he pulls that silver-case watch of his out and opens it up. He squints at that bear swinging back and forth and he looks down at his watch, up at the bear, down at his watch. And he says, Boys, if this-here old watch of mine is still keeping right, that bear is swinging just . . . a mite . . . slow. . . .

"Just a mite slow?" My father frowned. "I don't get it. A bear is not hanging in a tree to be keeping time. What does he mean, a mite slow?"

But that was the end of the story, and the end too of Uncle Zeno's talk. He only told stories, he didn't answer questions. The voice he listened to, the voice beyond the world, gave him only stories to report; any other matter was irrelevant. Uncle Zeno turned to my father but his gaze was so abstracted that the chair my father sat in at the supper table might as well have been empty.

That was part of the trouble. Uncle Zeno lived in a different but contiguous sphere that touched our world only by means of a sort of metaphysical courtesy. So how was he able to tell stories? He seemed to absorb reality, events that took place among people, without having to be involved.

"Was Homer blind because he was a poet?" my father asked me next day. "Or was he a poet because he was blind?"

"I don't know what you mean."

"I'm thinking about Uncle Zeno," he said.

"Oh," I said.

"You remember I told you the story of the *Iliad*? Well, Homer couldn't have been a soldier, of course, because he was blind. That's how he came to know so much. If he'd been a soldier, he couldn't have told the story. If Uncle Zeno ever struck a lick of work, if he ever had any dealings with people at all, maybe he couldn't tell his stories."

I could recall vividly my father's retelling of the *Iliad*. He found a magazine photograph of Betty Grable and propped it on the mantelpiece by the gilt pendulum clock and said that Miss Grable was Helen of Troy and had been stolen away by a slick-hair drugstore cowboy named Paris. Were we going to stand for that? Hell no. We were going to round up a posse and sail the wine-dark seas and rescue her. He flung himself down on the sagging sofa to represent Achilles loafing in his tent, all in a sulk over the beautiful captive maiden Briseis. He winked at me. "These women can sure cause a lot of trouble." The account ended ten minutes later with my father dragging three times around the room a dusty sofa cushion which was the vanquished corpse of Hector.

His excitement enticed me to read the poem in a Victorian prose translation, and I found it less confusing than his redaction, its thrills ordered.

That was the trouble with my father's storytelling. He was unable to keep his hands off things. Stories passed through Uncle Zeno like the orange glow through an oil-lamp chimney, but my father must always be seizing objects and making them into swords, elephants, and magic millstones, and he loved to end his stories with quick, violent gestures intended to startle his audience. He startled us, all right, but never by the power of his stories, always by the sharpness of his violence.

He had grown jealous of Uncle Zeno's storytelling and decided he would tell a suppertime story involving a mysterious house and a haunted shotgun. But his brief tale was so perplexed that we couldn't follow it at all. We were, however, disagreeably shocked when the haunted shotgun fired, because he illustrated this detonation with a swift blow of his fist on the edge of the table which caused the insert prongs of the inner leaf to break off, catapulting a bowl of butter beans onto my father's shirtfront.

My mother and grandmother and I stared at him in consternation as he mumbled and began plucking beans from his lap, but Uncle Zeno, sitting directly across the table, took no notice, gazing past my father's downcast confusion into his portable Outer Space. "That puts me in mind of . . ." he began, and proceeded to tell of a haunted house of his knowledge, atop which the weather vane pointed crosswise to the wind, in which fires flamed up without human agency in the fireplaces, and the cellar resounded with a singing chorus of lost children. We turned with grateful relief from my father's predicament and were soon enrapt by Uncle Zeno's monotone narrative, which now began to include sealed doors that sweated blood, a bathtub that filled up with copperhead snakes from the faucet, a vanity mirror that gave back the images of the dead, a piano whose keys turned to fangs whenever "Roses of Picardy" was attempted. My father too became enthralled and sat motionless among his butter beans until Uncle Zeno concluded. His ending, if that is the correct term, was, "Anyhow—"

That jerked my father awake. "Anyhow?" he cried. "What kind of climax is that? Did this Willie Hammer ever find the forbidden treasure or didn't he?"

But Uncle Zeno was not to speak again until possessed by another story, and he merely looked at my father with an expression of vacant serenity. My father gave up in disgust and began again to drop his lapful of beans into the bowl one at a time, plunk plunk plunk.

His jealousy grew. He was going to learn to tell stories that would shade Uncle Zeno's the way a mountain over-towers a hill of potatoes. He ransacked his memory, and he begged stories from the loafers down at Virgil Camp-bell's grocery store, and he began to delve into the vol-umes of fairy tales and folklore scattered about the house. He borrowed my book of Norse mythology and com-mitted a good half of it to memory. All to no avail. My father was simply too entranced with mischief and ef-fect, and the stories he managed to begin in leisurely fashion soon careered into wild gesticulation and ended with an unpleasant loud noise. "Wham!" he would shout. "I've gotcha!"

But he didn't have us, not in the way he wanted to, and he looked into our startled faces with an expression of expectancy quickly sagging to disappointment. "Well, maybe I left out some stuff," he would say, "but it's still a damn good story. Better than some I've heard lately."

Uncle Zeno said: That puts me in mind of Buford Rhodes and his coonhounds. Buford was a good old boy anyway you want and kind of crazy about raising coon-hounds and was an awful smart hand at it. Lived out there in Sudie's Cove in a tin-roof shack with his wife and six younguns and must have been a good dozen dogs. All kinds of dogs, Walkers and Blue Ticks and Redbones and lots of old hounds with the breeding mixed in like juices in soup. One of them named Raymond you couldn't never figure out, must have been a cross between a bloodhound and a Shetland pony. Kids rode that dog all day like a pony, he was that good-natured.

But it was the dog called Elmer that Buford was most proudest of, though Elmer wasn't much bred either, just an old sooner dog. Still he was the brightest dog anybody ever heard tell of. Buford was selling his hides to Sears and Roebuck for a dollar apiece. He'd catch them coons by the score and skin them and tack their hides up to cure. Got so after a while there wasn't a inch of wall on Buford's house or milkshed not covered with coon hides. So Buford always kept an eye out for old scrap lumber and kept piling it underneath his house to cure them hides on.

That was where Elmer's smartness come in. That dog Elmer was so smart that if Buford showed him a piece of oak board or a joint of pine siding, he'd take off and tree a coon which when the hide was skinned off and stretched would exactly fill out that length of wood. That was what made him so smart and valuable and caused Buford to think the world of him, rather have Elmer than the jewels of Sheba and the wisdom of Solomon.

But then they got into trouble one Tuesday about the middle of September. Elmer happened to wander inside the house while Buford was off somewhere and his wife had left the door open by mistake. Buford wouldn't never of let him in, ruins a good dog to lay around in a dwelling house. But Elmer wandered in this time and seen Buford's wife there ironing the laundry. He took one look at that ironing board and just lit out down the road as fast as he could go and heading west as far as you could point. Buford said later on he didn't know whether Elmer already had a coon that big somewhere he knew about or it just sparked his ambitions.

Whatever, Elmer had set hisself a journey and when Buford got home and heard what happened he took off after him. Dog like Elmer, that smart, can't afford to lose a dog like that. So Buford was traveling west now, trying to track him down, asking questions of anybody he came to, and for a long time he could tell where he'd been. Folks will remember a dog that's got something on its mind. But then the houses got scarcer and not many people to ask, and Buford was getting worried—

My father nodded sagely. "And I'll bet you're not going to tell us any more. You're just going to leave it hanging there, aren't you, Uncle Zeno?"

Uncle Zeno gazed into his placid abyss.

My father leaned over the table toward him. "Well, I've got your number now. I don't know any Willie Hammer or Lacey Joe Blackman or Setback Williams or those other people you've been telling us about. But it happens that I do know Buford Rhodes. Hired him one time to do some house painting. I know right where he lives, down there on Iron Duff, and I can drive right to his house. That's what I'm going to do, Uncle Zeno, and check your story out."

This possibility made no impression upon the old man. Why should it? We didn't care whether the story was true and Uncle Zeno didn't care about anything. But the idea that he could actually track down Buford Rhodes and talk to him seemed to give my father gleeful satisfaction.

It occurred to me that my father was preoccupied with the problem of Homer's blindness. Homer had lived in history and told his stories about real soldiers and described in grisly detail battles he could not have seen. But, like Uncle Zeno, Homer had left no trace in the world. Patient scholars were forced to debate whether the poet had actually ever lived. My father was not much interested in getting the details straight about coonhounds; he wanted to see if Buford Rhodes had ever met and talked to Uncle Zeno. The old man was living with us, eating our food and sleeping in the upstairs bedroom, but he was hardly present except as a voice. Like Homer, he was leaving no trace.

And so my father, in the disinterested pursuit of knowledge, was going to interview Buford Rhodes, the actual subject of one of Uncle Zeno's stories. Schliemann, unearthing the first traces of a Trojan site, must have felt something of the excitement my father felt.

My grandmother muttered that it seemed pure foolishness to her, traipsing down to Iron Duff for no good reason, but my father, leaning back in his chair and blowing a happy smoke ring, said, "That's just exactly where I'm headed first thing tomorrow morning."

Actually, he didn't get under way until midmorning, some five hours after rosy-fingered Dawn had streaked the sky with orient pearl and gold. I realize now that he had other necessary errands to perform, but of course he wouldn't give my grandmother the satisfaction of knowing he was doing something useful. He preferred for her to think he was off lollygagging after Uncle Zeno's story.

His absence left me with idle time and, since it was a lovely August morning and not yet sweltering, I decided to forgo reading and wander the hills of the farm until lunchtime. A favorite place for lonesome cowboy games was in a glade behind one of the farther hills of the pasture. An awesome storm had blown over a great oak tree there and I loved to clamber among the fallen branches and look at the jagged tears wrought in the trunk and see what new animal life had come to inhabit.

But when I arrived I found the tree already occupied. Uncle Zeno was sitting perched in an easy place on a big limb. His back was toward me and over his left shoulder protruded the end of the gnarly staff he sometimes used for walking. Never had his figure seemed so insignificant, his shoulders slumped and his head craned forward away from me so that I knew he was once again looking deep into his private void.

He was talking too, out here in the grassy knolls under the soft blue sky where there was not a living soul he could have been aware of to listen to him. I crept up as noiselessly as I could. I wanted to hear what he told himself in private, thinking that maybe the old man was revealing secrets of the earth he alone was privy to.

Here is what Uncle Zeno was saying:—but finally he was lost and he had to admit it. Hated it like poison, he'd never been lost in the woods before and he was hoping none of his buddies would ever hear about it, Buford Rhodes lost in the woods. He had give up on his good dog Elmer and he thought he'd be lucky if he could get back alive hisself. But right then he heard a baying he knew was Elmer and he begun to take heart. Happened though that he was down in a box cove with steep flanks on both sides and an anxious-looking rock-face cliff at the upper end. The sun was a-going down and the moon not coming up yet. And it echoed in there till he couldn't say where the baying was coming from. He started climbing, but by the time he was halfway up the mountainside Elmer lost the scent and hushed. Or maybe Elmer wasn't following no scent, just lost and worrying about it like Buford, but anyhow he shut up and not another sound out of him.

So now Buford was loster than before. He was going to swaller his pride and call for help, but he seen they wasn't no use, he wasn't close to nothing but mossy rocks and sawbriars. He set down there on a rotten pine log and he was feeling about as bad as a man can feel.

Didn't know how long he set there. It got cooler and the moon come up, turning the green leaves as white as snow, and it was as quiet as the bottom of a well. And then he seen somebody, or he thought he seen somebody, the moonlight deceiving. It was a Indian woman. She come at him smiling with her arms down at her sides, and he was awful happy to see her except when he tried to talk he found out she didn't speak nothing but Cherokee, which he didn't speak none of, not a speck. They tried to talk together but soon had to give it up as a bad job. She finally just reached out and took his hand and led him off with her, deeper and deeper into the woods, Buford feeling worse and worse. He was content he'd go with her wherever she wanted, he couldn't do no better.

It was a cave she lived in that she took him to and wasn't a bad cave, nice and dry, with some crevices for smoke to get out, and there was stuff to eat, berries and roots and herbs and squirrel meat. Wasn't the most comfortable place in the world but must have suited old Buford all right because he lived there in that cave with that Indian woman two year or more. Turned out not such a bad life after all, because Cherokee women don't like for their menfolks to do no work, and Buford just laid around and let her wait on him hand and foot. Ever once in a while at night he'd hear that fine hound dog Elmer start up baying somewhere off in the dark and Buford would get up and go scouring around the ridges, thrashing through blackberry briars and laurel hells. But then after a few months he didn't even bother to get up and look, didn't see much point in it anymore.

Went along like that two whole years, till one morning in spring he happened to wake up just when the woman was stepping over him to poke up the fire for breakfast and he took notice of a part of her he hadn't looked at close before and he wasn't what you call pleasured. Looked like a big ole crow had swallered a redbird there. He shut his eyes, and laying there with his eyes shut it come to him how awful ugly this woman was. He never thought about that before and now it started to bother him right much. After breakfast he sneaked away to a clearing where he had a favorite sandstone rock that he liked to sit on and think.

He set there and thought till he was pure gloomy. Here he was, lost in the woods and living with the ugliest woman creation ever made and he couldn't even talk to her. Well, he had plumb sunk into being a forsaken savage, all there was to it. Seemed to him there wasn't no hope for Buford Rhodes in this world anymore, he was lost to the sight of God and mankind. It was a black study he was in, but just right then when he was thinking his darkest thoughts, he heard a rustling over in the bushes—

At this point Uncle Zeno ceased. The story impulse had died in him, or maybe this story flew from this roosting-place across the world to another storyteller, Chinese or Tibetan, who sat waiting for inspiration. Uncle Zeno's audience—the white clouds and fallen tree, the blue daylight and sweet green grass—listened patiently, but the story was over for now. Yet here in the glade was the best setting for his stories, and I felt that I understood him in a way I hadn't before. He was some necessary part of nature we hadn't recognized, seeing him only as a windy old man. But he was more than that, and different. What was he doing now that the story had ended in him? Why, he was sitting on the tree, giving audience to the history of its regal life and calamitous downfall, a story I couldn't hear. I would have to wait until Uncle Zeno was possessed by the impulse to repeat it to us.

I hoped he would never find out I'd been there to over-hear him. I turned away quietly and went back to the house and made a lunch of bread and cheese and butter-milk from the icebox. I ate alone. My mother and grand-mother had walked over to pay their respects to a shut-in friend, my father was down in Iron Duff playing archeologist-detective, and Uncle Zeno was in the pasture telling stories to the mica rocks and horse nettles.

After lunch I took a book of science out to the porch to read, learning that Sirius was the most luminous star in our heavens and was thought in old times to bring on madness in people and fits of poetic frenzy. I didn't care to read fiction; I'd had enough stories for a while.

My father returned about four o'clock and came to the porch to sit and chat with me. He looked haggard.

"What did you find out?" I asked him.

He rubbed the back of his neck and looked at the pine ceiling. His tone was mournful, puzzling. "Nothing," he said.

"Couldn't you find Buford Rhodes?"

"Couldn't find him, couldn't find anyone who knew him, couldn't find the least trace of him."

"Maybe you went to the wrong house. You might have forgot where he lived."

"Drove right to his front door, where he used to live. House was empty and run-down. Windows broken, doors off the hinges. Holes in the roof. Looked like nobody had lived in it for twenty years."

"Did you ask the neighbors?"

"They never heard of him. Walked down to Hipps' gro-cery, and nobody there ever heard of him either."

"You must have got the wrong place. Somebody would know him."

"I drove down to ask Virgil Campbell. He knows every-body that was ever in the county. At first he thought he sort of did remember a Buford Rhodes, but the more he thought about it the less he could remember."

"Maybe you got the name mixed up," I said. "Maybe the man you hired to paint had a name like that but different."

"I know Buford Rhodes," he said. "Know him anywhere. Uncle Zeno described him to a T." He snapped his fingers. "I'm glad you mentioned that. I recall I paid Buford with a check. I'll have a record in my check stubs. Paid him seventy-seven dollars exactly. Wasn't but three years ago, I'll go look that up." He rose and walked to the door.

"Where did you eat dinner?" I asked.

He gave me another harried look. "I haven't been hungry lately, Jess," he said and went in to pore through his records.

But this research, too, proved disappointing. He found a check stub for the amount of seventy-seven dollars, and its date would fit into the period of the house painting, but he had failed to list whom he'd written the check to.

When the women returned from their errand of charity he asked my mother about it. "See, here's the check stub," he said, waving it under her chin. "You remember Buford Rhodes, don't you?"

She backed away from the flapping paper. "We had three or four painters working about that time. I don't remember any of them."

"You'd remember Buford, though. Had the kind of beard that gives you a blue face. Always cracking jokes and talking about his hound dogs. Always had a drink or two under his belt no matter what time of day it was."

"That describes every house painter I ever met," she said.

"You ought to remember him, though. Uncle Zeno has got him down exactly. He was some kind of character."

"All I ever meet are characters," she said. "I don't believe that normal human beings show up in this part of the country."

Exasperated, he flung down the booklet of stubs and stamped on it. "How could anybody not remember Buford Rhodes?" he shouted.

"Calm down," she said. "It's not important."

But it was important to my father, and his shouting indicated the intensity of his feelings. I almost spoke

up then. I almost told him that the last I'd heard Buford
Rhodes was lost in the forest and living in a cave with
an ugly Indian woman. I realized, however, that I had
better not speak; this information would only cause
more confusion.

I was assailed by a wild thought and a goosy sensation.
What if Buford Rhodes had ceased to exist upon the earth
because Uncle Zeno told stories about him? I had entertained odd fancies since overhearing the old man this
morning. What if Uncle Zeno's stories so thoroughly absorbed the characters he spoke of that they took leave of
the everyday world and just went off to inhabit his nar-
ratives? Everything connected with them would disap-
pear, they would leave no more sign among us than a
hawk's shadow leaves in the snow he flies above. The
only place you could find Achilles these days was in the
Iliad. Had he ever existed otherwise? Had any of those
heroes left evidence behind?

I cried out, "What about Agamemnon?"

My father gave me a peculiar look. "What about him?"

"Didn't you tell me they found his death mask? Didn't
you say it was a mask made out of gold and they put it in
a museum?"

He answered in a vexed tone. "That's the name
they give it, but they can't really prove it belonged to
Agamemnon."

"Well, it ain't his," I said. "They've got the wrong man."
Because now I was convinced of my notion. Homer and
Uncle Zeno did not merely describe the world, they used
it up. My father said that one reason Homer was reckoned such a top-notch poet was that you couldn't tell
where the world left off and the *Iliad* began. . . No wonder you couldn't tell.

My theory was wild enough to amuse my father; it
was just the sort of mental play-pretty he liked to entertain himself with. But I decided not to tell him about it.
He was earnestly troubled by the problem of Buford
Rhodes and obviously in no mood for metaphysical specu-
lations in the philosophy of narrative. I could read that

much on his face. Then he said, "Come on, Jess. We'd better get the milking chores done."

I rose and followed him willingly. I looked forward to getting the evening chores out of the way and sitting down to supper. I was hungry, with nothing but bread and cheese for lunch, and I was eager to hear Uncle Zeno tell another story. I felt like a scientist now that I'd hit upon my brilliant idea, and I wanted to watch the process at work.

Sure enough, as soon as my grandmother had got through one of her painfully detailed supper prayers, Uncle Zeno began talking, without excuse or preamble, as always.

—and out of the bushes there, Uncle Zeno said, come a gang of six kids, looked to be eight, ten years old, and dressed in washed overalls and pinafores. They kept staring at Buford and he begun to think for the first time how he might look awful strange, dirty and bearded from living in the woods so long. But he kept hisself soft-talking and gentled them kids along until they agreed to lead him back to civilization. These here kids belonged to the Sunday-school class of a hard-shell Baptist church back up that way and they'd run into Buford while they was hunting Easter eggs. Turned out he hadn't been as lost as he thought he was, no more than two miles from a little old settlement there, and the congregation had come up here for an Easter picnic. It was just that Buford's mind had been occupied, thinking about that Indian woman and worrying about his good dog Elmer that he hadn't heard bay in more than a year now. Buford just hadn't been taking no proper interest, that was all.

So the kids led him out of the woods down to the settlement and he got started on the right road a-going home. He was dreading to arrive, figured his place must have gone to rack and ruin while he was gone and his wife and children probably in the poorhouse a long time ago. He didn't know what he was going to tell folks and whether anybody would believe him or not.

But when he came in sight of his house, well, he was

mighty surprised. The place was all fixed up and just a-shining, better than he ever done for it. There was a spanking new tin roof, and them old coon hides had been tore down from everywhere and the house was painted up nice and white and there was a new Ford car setting by the edge of the yard.

So he reckoned his wife had took up with another man while he was gone and they wouldn't have no use for him around there no more. But he went on up anyhow and rapped at the door. It took his wife a minute or two to recognize him but when she did she was happy fit to bust and hugged him tight and his kids run out in fine new clothes and jumped around, it was the best welcome-home you'd ever want to see.

After they settled down a little bit he got to questioning her. How come you're doing so good, with the house all fixed up and a Ford car in the front yard? And she said it was Elmer. Elmer had found his way finally back home a year ago and seen how the family was doing poorly, so he went out and got hisself a job. Buford said that was awful good news, he was proud of that dog, and what kind of job did he have. She said Elmer got him a job teaching over at the high school, arithmetic and natural science, and drawed a pretty good salary considering he didn't have no experience to speak of. And Buford said a dog that smart didn't need no experience, what he was going to do was get Elmer to show him how to smell the ground and track coon and they'd switch off, Buford would be the dog and Elmer could be the man because maybe that's the way it ought to have been in the first place—

"All right," my father said. "I'm glad to hear some more of that story." He kept rubbing the back of his neck. "But what I want to know is, Where does Buford live now? I've been looking for him all day and can't turn up hide nor hair. Speak, Uncle Zeno. Tell us where Buford Rhodes has got to."

But of course there was no answer. Uncle Zeno looked calmly into his vast inane, contemplating the nothingness that hung between stories. He probably wasn't aware that my father spoke to him. He lifted a slow spoonful of creamed corn to his mouth.

My father leaned back, his sensibilities sorely bruised. "No, you're not going to tell us. I know that. I wish I hadn't asked." He heaved a sorrowful sigh and looked down at his lap. "Well, now I'll tell a story," he said. "It's my turn." He leaned forward again, placing the palms of both hands flat on the table, and stared intently into Uncle Zeno's face. He looked like a bobcat ready to spring. "Once upon a time there was a pretty good old boy who never did anybody any harm. I won't say his name, but he was a pretty good old boy. It happened that he fell in love with a fine mountain girl and married into her family and they lived there in the hills and he worked the farm for them. That was all right, everything was just fine. Except that in this family there was an army of strange uncles who were always dropping by, and they were an interesting bunch, most of them. This good old boy—let's just call him Joe—got along O.K. with these strange visitors. He liked to talk to them and find out about them. He was interested, you know, in what makes people tick. . . . But there was this one weird uncle— we'll call him Uncle Z.—he couldn't figure out to save his life. Truly he couldn't. And it began to prey on his mind until he couldn't make himself think about anything but this Uncle Z. and how queer he was. . . . I'm sorry to tell you, Uncle Zeno, that I don't know the end of this story. But I think that this good old boy started worrying so much that he finally just went crazy and they carried him off to the funny farm in a straitjacket." He gazed morosely into the plate of food he had hardly touched. "But like I say, I don't really know the end of the story."

My grandmother reprimanded him, in a tone gentler than usual. "Now, Joe Robert, you don't want to be unmannerly."

He stood up. "No, of course I don't," he said. "If you-all will excuse me, I think I'll go out on the porch and have a cigarette. Maybe clear my head. I don't know what's the matter with me." He fumbled a moment with the knob, then stepped through the door and closed it.

My mother and grandmother looked at each other, and my grandmother said, "Joe Robert's acting kind of peculiar, seems to me. He ain't ailing, is he?"

"He doesn't seem to be ill," my mother said.

"It's Uncle Zeno's stories," I told them. "They get him all worked up. He wants to do something, but he don't know what to do."

"They're only stories," my mother said. "No one is supposed to do anything *about* them."

I wanted to reply, but I couldn't very well tell my mother that she didn't understand my father, that he always had to be doing things, changing the order of the world in some way, causing anarchy when he could or simple disorder if he couldn't do any better.

"Just seems peculiar to me," my grandmother said, "somebody getting all worked up about a few harmless windies." She looked at our visitor with a fond expression. "Why, Uncle Zeno wouldn't harm a fly."

The three of us gazed at him, an inoffensive old man who hardly seemed to occupy the chair he sat in. He seemed ignorant of our regard, and it was clear that what she said was true. He wouldn't harm a fly.

Then his drifting abstraction formed into a voice and he began to speak again. "That puts me in mind of," Uncle Zeno said, "Cousin Annie Barbara Sorrells that lived down toward the mouth of Ember Cove. Had a right nice farm there, about a hundred acres or so, but didn't have nobody to work it, her oldest son dying when he was eight and her other boy, Luden, gone off to California on a motorcycle. But she had her a son-in-law, Joe Robert his name was, and he was a pretty fair hand at farming, she didn't have no complaints to speak of, except that Joe Robert was ever the sort to dream up mischief. . . . Well, it happened one time that her boy Luden had sent Annie Barbara a present, which was a box of fancy candies he'd bought in St. Louis—"

This was too much.

Uncle Zeno was telling a story about us. I knew what he was going to say; I'd lived through those events, after all. His story focused on my father, and that fact disturbed me. My father didn't seem to get along too well with Uncle Zeno as it was, and perhaps he wouldn't be happy to hear that he was now a character in the old man's stories.

I jumped up without even saying Excuse me and went out to the porch. It was as dark as the dreams of a sleeping bear; rain clouds blocked off the starlight and there was only a dim light coming through the dining room drapes. My father was not smoking, but just sitting in a chair shoved flat against the wall of the house.

"Are you here?" I asked.

He paused a long time before answering. "Yeah, I'm right here, Jess."

"Are you feeling O.K.?"

Another pause, and I could hear Uncle Zeno's mumble drone through the door.

"I'm all right, I guess. Maybe I'm catching a cold. I've been feeling kind of light-headed. Feel a little weak all over, like I'd lost a lot of weight in a hurry."

"Come on back in and have a piece of apple pie. Maybe it'll make you feel better."

He sat motionless. There was no wind sound, no sound at all except for the low, indistinct mutter of Uncle Zeno's story.

"Apple pie," he said softly. "Well, that's not bad medicine." He didn't move for a while yet. Finally he rose slowly from the chair. But when he took a step he walked directly into darkest shadow and I couldn't see him at all and at that moment Uncle Zeno's story concluded and all the night went silent.

Seven / *The Maker of*
One Coffin

When Uncle Runkin came to visit he brought his coffin
and slept in it, laying it across a couple of sawhorses we
carried into the upstairs bedroom. But I could never imagine him sleeping. If I crept in at midnight, wouldn't I find
him with his bony hands crossed on his chest and his
weird eyes staring, staring into the dark? I didn't care to
find out; I was frightened of him, and maybe my father
was too at first, though he'd never let on. He treated
Uncle Runkin lightly, loosely, banteringly, but surely he
was bemused by our odd visitor who must have spent
the majority of his years preparing to lie forever in his
cold grave.

We often hosted wandering aunts and uncles, all on
my mother's side, and they intrigued my father endlessly
and he was always glad when one of them showed up to
break the monotony of a mountain farm life. Especially
glad for Uncle Runkin; he had a reputation which pre-
ceded him as twilight precedes darkness, and we were
not to be disappointed.

He was slight, about five foot eight, and frail looking
because he carried no fat and not much muscle. "All
skin and bones"; Uncle Runkin was the only person I
ever met who fit the description. The bones in his hands

and head were starkly prominent beneath parchment-colored skin as tight on him as a surgeon's glove. His head was entirely hairless, and not pink but yellowish. His beaky nose drooped sharply. His eyes were black as coffee grounds and large and sunken in his skull and surrounded by large circles as dark as the great pupils. These eyes looked quite past you, and Uncle Runkin made you feel he saw you without looking; and that was another unsettling sensation.

His motions were grave and deliberate and I never saw him smile. His skin was dry as wood shavings and when he touched any surface there was a slight raspy whisper, like a rat stirring in a leaf pile. Or like a copperhead snake skinning over the edge of a table. Or like a black silk pall sliding off a coffin. I never got used to it; each time I heard it was like looking down into a bottomless well.

I never got used to anything about Uncle Runkin. It wasn't that he tried to discomfit us; I think indeed that he tried not to. But whenever I was in his presence I felt like I was standing with my back to a cliff and couldn't remember where the edge was.

The same uneasiness affected my father, but he hid it pretty well. He teased Uncle Runkin and joked, but it was easier to be sociable with the midnight wind. His jollity went out into the void and no laughter returned. And we were not certain we wanted to hear the kind of laughter that might return; it wouldn't be what you call comradely.

Still my father kept on, gibing and bantering ever more recklessly, his gestures growing ever more strained and awkward. Waving his hands about at the supper table, he tipped over the salt shaker.

Uncle Runkin gave the spilled salt a solemn glance and uttered his most characteristic sentence. "That means that somebody is going to die."

"What? Spilling the salt?" my father said. His desperation was obvious now; he snatched up the shaker and began sprinkling salt all over the green tablecloth. "Fine and dandy," he said. "We'll do away with the whole German army."

"It never is somebody you'd want to die," Uncle Runkin said.

My father gave him a wild look. "Well then, who? Who's going to kick the bucket?"

But he didn't answer; his voice box had silted up again with crematory ashes.

Uncle Runkin found lots of signs for coming death. A black cat crossing in front of you, the new moon seen over your left shoulder, a flock of crows taking flight on your lefthand side, one crow flying against the full moon, sunset reflected in a window of a deserted house, an owl hooting just at dark, a ladder leaning oddly in a corner, the timbers of our old house creaking at night: he knew all these as indications that somebody was going to die, and the way he said *somebody* made you want to reconsider your plans for airplane trips and bear hunts.

My father scoffed. "It would take Noah's flood and the Black Plague to carry off as many victims as he's seen signs for." But I could hear in his voice a shaky bravado.

Uncle Runkin's silly prognostications affected us all, but me—eleven years old—most. I found myself calculating where the new moon was in relation to my left shoulder, and I wouldn't look at the full moon because who knows when the crows might fly? And I began to operate mighty gingerly with the salt shaker. . . . He affected us in other ways as well. I'd never remembered my dreams before, but after Uncle Runkin arrived I couldn't forget them, much as I wanted to.

I thought he would say No, but when I asked to look at his coffin he seemed pleased I was interested. Coffin or no, it was an impressive piece of handiwork, though a monstrous huge thing, as we'd discovered in wrestling it up the stairs. Eight feet long and four feet wide, it was much too large for Uncle Runkin, and he must have lain lonesome in it like a single pearl in a jewel case. The corners were so tightly mitered and joined that I could hardly find the seams with my fingertip. The wood, he told me proudly, came from an enormous black walnut, and the bottom and sides of the coffin were cut from whole slabs. There was a triple molding as elegant as ever you could see at the base of the coffin, and an elaborate cornice at the top with a crisp dentate design. The lid was to be attached with no fewer than eight brass butterfly hinges, and he looked forward to its completion.

It wasn't complete because the lid wasn't finished. Handsome as the box was, it wasn't a patch on what the lid was going to be. The unfinished lid sat on the long worktable out in our woodshed, covered with two blankets of heavy green felt and the weathered old tarpaulin he secured the coffin in when he hauled it in his open pickup truck.

He peeled the wrappings back so I could have a look at his hand carving. Along the edges ran a garland of grapes and apples, roses and lilies, intricately intertwined and delicately incised, down to the leaf veins. In the center was a largish death's-head, and it was interesting how much this skull resembled a self-portrait, only having an ominous hole where he had a beaky nose. Otherwise it was Uncle Runkin to the life. Or death. There was a blank entablature below on which he was going to engrave a motto, as soon as he could decide whether it was to be *Come lovely Angel* or *Sweet Death comes to Soothe* or *How glorious our Final Rest*. Or a phrase that destiny hadn't yet thrown in his way. He was still searching out mottoes. Beneath the blank he'd carved what he called a sleeping lamb, which looked to me like it would dream no more forever. Not quite completed, though the great work had taken him twenty-five years so far. The lid alone cost him seven years, but easy to see it was going to be worth it, rubbed and oiled and varnished and polished until it was as smooth as the inside of an eggshell and dark and satiny.

My father suggested that the motto ought to be *Death, where you been all my life?* But he too admired the coffin and complimented Uncle Runkin. Later he changed his motto suggestion to *Opus 1* because, he said, making that coffin was the sole lick of work the old man had ever struck.

We talked about Uncle Runkin sleeping in his coffin, and we tried to imagine what that would be like. I thought it would be scary but exciting, and I didn't think it would be stuffy in there, but as cool and dark as eternity. I imagined that after you got accustomed to it, you would have peaceful winter dreams and hear voices from beyond the grave.

"What do you think the dead folks are saying?" my father asked.

"I don't know," I said. "I can't imagine that part. What do you think they're saying?"

"I don't know," he said. "But every time I imagine lying in the grave my ass starts to itch."

I wanted to try it. I wanted to sneak into Uncle Runkin's room some hour when he was away and lie down in the coffin and see what I thought about it.

"I wouldn't do it," my father said. "I'm no great believer in signs, but there can't be much good luck in lying around in coffins all the time. I don't much look forward to death myself; it's like knowing you have to go to the dentist."

"I don't think it's like that. I think it would be real quiet." (I made noise in the company of dentists.)

"Well, if quiet is what you desire, you're going to have a riproaring time after you're gone. The graveyard eats up noise like Uncle Runkin eats his supper."

I knew what he meant. Uncle Runkin cleaned his plate so thoroughly that it was surprising to see the design still on it, the little blue Chinese bridge with the lumpy tree and long necked bird. Everything was gone, including the chicken bones, and not even a smear of grease remained. But I never saw him eat, never use a knife or fork or spoon. The plate would be steaming full before him and then the first time I noticed, it would be spotless, and Uncle Runkin wouldn't be chewing but looking at me, or rather beyond me, with unearthly speculation.

"I know what we can do," my father said. "We can steal that coffin."

"What in the world for?"

"Don't you have any curiosity? I'd just like to see what the old man would do when he couldn't find it."

I had mixed feelings about the idea. It was all right to look at the coffin and even to touch it, but when I thought about stealing it, it took a different shape in my mind. Became bigger and blacker and heavier and deeper. I felt we would be tampering with dark forces we knew nothing about, distressing some of the bones of the universe. "I'm not so sure," I said.

"Why not?"

"Too heavy," I said. "The three of us like to never wallered it up the stairs. Two of us wouldn't get it to budge an inch."

"I guess you're right," he said. "I'll think of something, though."

"Maybe you oughtn't to. Maybe Uncle Runkin is one uncle we ought to leave plumb alone."

"Yeah?" He gave me an amused look. "That old man hasn't got you buffaloed, has he, Jess?"

"He's a different kind of uncle from what we're used to."

"Don't worry," he said. "I just now figured out what we'll do." But when he chuckled softly, I had to feel uneasy.

I don't know what supernatural spell my father was able to exercise over my mother. It had to be one of nearly unthinkable power for her to aid him. Probably there was nothing more sinister about it than the fact that she too had a sense of mischief, usually dormant, which he was able to arouse on urgent and suitable occasions.

And this occasion was, for my father, an urgent one. The family had undergone gradual but significant changes since Uncle Runkin came. There was less casual talk, less casual touching, and less laughter. We were not absorbed in gloom, all day thinking morose thoughts, but we had surely darkened and a quiet seriousness began to prevail over us.

It was just the sort of atmosphere my father couldn't abide, and he may well have felt that he was struggling for psychic survival.

Whatever means he used, they were successful. My mother brought home one Friday afternoon the skeleton from the health classroom at her high school. I know she didn't steal it; she wouldn't stray so far from the straight and narrow. Probably she just asked to borrow it for the weekend. "I don't know why," she would say. "My husband imagines he's got some use for it."

So we had a skeleton, and a lovely object it was too, properly wired together, all white and smooth, and its teeth intact. I was curious about where the high school had got hold of it, and my father said it was a former fullback on the Black Bears who had run the wrong way in a game and scored a safety for the Hiawassee Catamounts. "Huh," I said. He then told me it was a woman's skeleton, an axe murderess who had chopped up her mother-in-law, her husband, her eleven children, and the family poodle and then, realizing what she'd done, turned the axe on herself and committed suicide.

"I don't believe that one, either," I said.

"That's the difference between us and Uncle Runkin," my father said. "He would believe that story in a jiffy. And you know what he'd say?"

"He'd say, *In the midst of life we are in death.*"

"That's it exactly," my father said.

He had no very elaborate plans for the skeleton. He was merely going to lay it out in the coffin where Uncle Runkin slept. "That ought to give him something to think about." Then, as an afterthought, he decided to remove from the fuse box the fuse which controlled the upstairs bedroom lights so that Uncle Runkin would have to clump up in the dark to meet his unannounced bedfellow. "I'll tell him something's wrong with the wiring on that side, but that I'm working to fix it. Meanwhile, take every candle in the house and hide them."

125

This was one of my father's less complicated ruses, and the details were easily arranged. We ate our Saturday night supper in what had become our habitual bemused silence, and Uncle Runkin practiced his usual legerdemain, disappearing every scrap and nitlet of food from his plate. He took his whispery-silent leave of us to go up to his room. My father had already lied about the wiring, and we made an ostentatious search for the candles that I'd stuck away in a feed bin in the barn.

We couldn't hear our uncle, but we sat at the table without talking and felt his progress through the house on our skins. We knew when he opened the hallway door upon darkness and went touching his way down the hall. We knew when he mounted the first step of the stairs and grasped the banister in his dry hand. We could feel every step upward he took and the pause he made at the top in order to get his bearings in pitch darkness. We felt how he inched down the upstairs hall and opened the door to his room and slid in the dark over to the edge of the coffin and began to disrobe.

But after that we knew nothing. Our heightened senses and imaginations failed us at this critical point, and we couldn't say what would happen, but sat hushed, waiting.

We sat a long time in silence. We looked at one another. I don't know what we expected from Uncle Runkin, a bloodcurdling scream, or a crash and shouted curses, or maybe the sight of the old man fleeing naked and bony-shanked out into the October night. Now it seems unlikely that we would have been treated to any of these edifying spectacles; the old man's attachment to the Black Deliverer was more profound than we could fathom, and there was nothing about death that was going to surprise him.

We sat a long time.

Finally my mother said, "Well, Joe Robert, this is one of your little pranks that didn't work out."

He sighed. "I didn't care what. As long as *something* happened, I would have felt better."

"And after all the trouble I went to to get that pile of bones," she said. "You boys go right up to his room in the morning and get that skeleton. I'll be in hot water if I don't get it back to school first thing Monday."

"Yes ma'am," my father said. His voice rang hollow with defeat.

Next morning Uncle Runkin came down to breakfast, all polished and ready for church. He'd tracked down some minor sect of strange Baptists yon side of Turkey Knob, with a preacher who gave sermons on the utter and awful and final power of death over life, and this little cinder block church drew Uncle Runkin the way a rosebush draws Japanese beetles.

During breakfast my father made a couple of feeble attempts. "Did you sleep sound last night, Uncle Runkin?"

He answered Yes in that voice that was like a breath of dying desert wind.

"No trouble with bedbugs—or anything like that?"

He told us No in that same sepulchral voice and my father bent to his plate and took a mouthful of gloomy eggs.

After Uncle Runkin departed for church, my father pushed his chair back from the table and said, "Well, Jess, let's go up and rescue our skeleton." He looked as cheerless as a bloodhound.

Then it got worse because the skeleton was not there in the coffin. Nor anywhere else in the room. Nor in any other upstairs room, not in the bedroom, nor in the storage room, nor in the bathroom, nor in the attic above the storage room. And in no downstairs room. We searched and searched again every nook and corner of every room of the house, and there was no trace of it, not the least little finger bone.

"What in the world could he have done with it?" my father asked.

"I don't know," I said.

He looked at me with a glazed expression. "Look here, Jess, you don't think he ate it, do you?"

"I don't think so," I said, but I had to remember all the squirrel and rabbit and chicken and pork chop bones that were never left on Uncle Runkin's plate.

"I believe he did. I believe the old man ate that skeleton."

"Is that what you're going to tell Mama? So she can tell them at the high school that our uncle ate the skeleton from the health class?"

"I purely don't know," he said.

That was what she asked when she heard. "What am I going to tell them at the high school?"

"I think you'd better lie to them," my father said.

"Lie?" she wailed. "I can't lie to them. I don't know how."

"Nothing to it," he said. "We'll stay up late tonight and I'll teach you."

That afternoon Uncle Runkin made me go with him to look at a graveyard he had discovered. It was an old one, disused and grown up in weeds and sawbriars. Thick mosses and peeling lichen flooded the stones and some of the markers were just thin slabs of shale with the names and rude designs etched in with farm tools, cold chisels and axe bits and the like.

"What did we come here to see?" I asked.

He looked at me in surprise. "Why—everything," he said, and he swept the air to indicate the universe that interested him, the graves and weeds and briars and, I suppose, the grubs and worms munching away underground. "Don't you feel at peace here? Ain't it a shame people have let this beautiful spot go to ruin? Wouldn't this be an awful nice place if you wanted to build a house close by?"

Maybe it was beautiful, but for me it was a graveyard, and I wasn't ready to invest in that brand of real estate. Chill bumps rose on my forearms. "I don't know," I said.

"Let's go around and look at some of the stones," he said, and his voice was dreamy and intimate.

So that's what we did, with Uncle Runkin pausing before each hacked stone in rapt contemplation. He would stare at the stone, read off the inscription silently, stare at it some more, and then wag his head solemnly and pace up the hill to the next. He clasped his hands behind his back like a philosopher.

I wandered with him, feeling bored and dreary.

"Keep an eye out for any good motto I might could put on my coffin lid," he said.

"Well, how about this one here? *Gone but not forgotten.*"

"Look at the name on it," he said. "*Rodney Walsh. You ever hear of Rodney Walsh?*"

"No," I said, "but they buried him in 1910."

"You know any Walshes in this county?"

"No."

"Well, see, he's gone all right, but he's plumb forgotten too. You see that motto a lot, but it just ain't going to do. People don't remember you after you're dead. That's why you have to do it all yourself beforehand."

"How about this one?" I asked. "*She done what she could.*"

"Well, but don't that make it clear she done a right piddling job?"

"Here's one. *A brighter day awaits.*"

He snorted. "What they mean by that? Next Thursday?"

We meandered on among the markers, and each time I would read off the writing he would be right there with a telling critique. I finally had to admire his expertise; he'd pondered on it until he was a connoisseur. And I admired the way he never got depressed by it; in fact, the more gravestones we looked at, the mournfuller the inscriptions became, the better he liked it; and if it was anybody but Uncle Runkin I would have said he was bright and cheerful.

"*Gone to a better place,*" I read.

"How do they know that?" he said. "I bet this William Jennings done a whole lot of meanousness they just never heard about."

"Grave, where is thy victory?"

"Suppose this here where we're standing is the battle-field where death and the living had a fight. Who would you say won?"

"Gone to lighten the dark."

"Now that one might have possibilities," he said. "I'll be thinking about that one." He took a little notebook and carpenter's pencil out of his overalls bib and wrote it down. I thought he must have a hefty backlog of that kind of writing by now, and I was pretty sure it was his favorite reading matter, along with Job and the obituary page and the Lamentations of Jeremiah.

The motto he took the brightest shine to was, *In Life's full Prime Is Death's own Time;* he was positively gleeful when we struck on it and wrote it down and underscored it twice. "There's a lot of wisdom on these stones, if people would just take the opportunity," he said, and he was happy enough to be willing to leave for home, which didn't exactly break my heart.

At home he headed directly into the small room off the kitchen hallway where the coal stove and radio were. There was a radio program on Sunday afternoons called "Meditations" that he never missed. It was all slow organ music playing behind a fellow who read passages out of a book of dejected thoughts and it was just the thing to brace Uncle Runkin up.

I went upstairs, hoping against hope that I might lo-cate the lost skeleton, though I knew my father had searched the place over again while Uncle Runkin and I were out. I went into his room and poked about quietly, but found no trace of Mr. Bones. I was attracted at this moment by his imposing coffin there on the sawhorses and went over to it and laid my cheek against its smooth side to enjoy the cool and polish of the wood. I pulled up a chair and looked over into it, and now it seemed invit-ing, sweet and peaceful. I'd never been much interested in coffins before, but prolonged exposure to Uncle Run-kin had begun to change my outlook, and I thought it might not be such a bad thing to be dead, not having to get up on frosty mornings to milk crazy old cows, not having to learn multiplication or the capital of North Dakota, not having to eat cold fried grits when my grandmother felt trifling.

I tugged off my high-topped shoes and stepped over into the coffin and lay down. It was marvelous at first. The black satin plush was not cool, as I'd thought, but warm and soft; he'd cushioned it with cotton batting. The black plush sides rose up steep in my vision, giving me a view of the ceiling in a box, and the perspective caused me to feel I was sinking down and down, that the world outside was receding. I waited for the sensation to pass but it never did; the ceiling, the room, the house, the farm, the sky kept pulling back from my sight, floating away to some unreachable forever. And I began to think of the coffin as being like the bathysphere of William Beebe, except that the coffin sank not through water but through solid substance, would drop through the floor of the room, down through the foundations of the house, and dive into the earth; and I would be able to look upon creatures never seen or imagined before, animals made of glowing mineral that swam the veins of the world and traced their mysterious lives to mysterious destinies.

Then I fell asleep.

As soon as my eyes closed I was assaulted by a barrage of fleeting dream images. A sky full of stars arranged itself in an unreadable tombstone motto. A great silent galleon with black silk sails lifted off an ebony ocean and floated into the sky, straight into the full moon. A flock of crows flew through a snowstorm, then changed into a rain of blood and fell, staining the snowy ground scarlet. A sinister monk opened the orange-lit door in a mountain and stepped out; he was dressed in a loose black robe and made arcane gestures with his bony hands, causing a spiky crop of skeletons to rise out of the ground and giggle.

But none of these visions was frightening; they were comforting, and I began to know that death was the

131

Meadow of Vision, where dream was wrested from the marrow of stars.

One vision, though, was not comforting but disturbing. That was the sight of Death himself. In my dream I was standing in a narrow doorway, which had no building to belong to, in the middle of a barren plain. Nothing was before or behind me but blank wind. His pinched, intense face appeared suddenly out of the air, his sunken eyes burning dementedly, and he recognized me there in my constricting doorway and reached out his paw of lightning and caressed my cheek. I jerked and quivered from the shock of his touch, and yelled an awful yell, a soul-shaking screech.

Death yelled too and leapt back away from me, and it was obvious that he also had been frightened. Death and I had met face to face and scared the pee out of each other. And then it was obvious that I wasn't asleep and dreaming of Death and a doorway; instead, I was awake in Uncle Runkin's coffin and the old man, not expecting to find me there, had cried out in surprise. What he cried was *Yipes!*, just like Dagwood in the funny paper.

Yipes! That's the only time in my life I heard anyone say that word.

Then I heard Uncle Runkin rush out of the room and fly down the stairs. I sat up slowly, groggy from sleep and my harsh awakening, and took my time clambering out of the coffin and finding my shoes and putting them on in the dusk-dim room. From downstairs in the kitchen came the ruckus sound of heated conversation, and it was a sure thing that Uncle Runkin had not enjoyed finding me asleep in his coffin and was down there stirring up the family against me.

I sat in the straight chair and stared at the floor. I knew I was in for some kind of punishment, but I didn't care. I was dazed. After all, I had been out to visit the afterlife and had found it an entrancing place, and so a few licks with a hickory switch held no terror for me, and a month of Saturdays without cowboy movies not much disappointment. If death was as entertaining as it had been

132

there in the promise of the coffin, I could always hang myself and have forever a free show that was better than any cowboy movie.

The noise downstairs went on and on, and I sat there and looked at my shoes until the noise stopped and I heard my father and Uncle Runkin coming up the stairs. When they entered the room my father switched on the light and all the strange thoughts that had been bemusing my mind flew away like a flock of birds at a gunshot.

"Jess," my father said, "Uncle Runkin has decided he can't stay with us any longer. He's got some pressing business in hand and needs to move on."

"That so?" I said, and I looked at Uncle Runkin but he wouldn't look back. He went over to his coffin and smoothed out the plush where I had been lying and inspected all over the wood for damage.

"Yes, he says he's afraid he'll have to be leaving," my father said. "So if you wouldn't mind giving us a hand with the coffin."

"Not at all," I said. "Be glad to."

It was much less a chore to get the coffin down the stairs and out of the house than it had been to get it upstairs. We slid it onto the truckbed and Uncle Runkin went to the shed and got the lid and placed it carefully over the box. We left him there, blanketing his treasure and roping it down tight. We went in and sat at the kitchen table, and my father poured coffee for himself and my mother.

In a few minutes the old man came in. My father stood up and they shook hands. Then he turned to my mother and offered her a slow, dry half-bow. He gave me one soulful burning glance and then stepped out and closed the door and was gone. Didn't utter a syllable. We heard the truck start up.

My father sat down and sipped the coffee. He blinked his eyes. "Whew," he said. "*A load off my mind.* I never knew what that sentence meant till right this minute."

My mother and I nodded. The old brick house felt lighter around our shoulders now that coffin was out of it.

"I have to admit I feel better too," she said.

My father yawned and stretched. "I don't know about you-all," he said, "but Uncle Runkin kind of took it out of me. I think I'll mosey on to bed, no matter how early it is."

That sounded good to me too, even though I'd already had a nice nap not so long ago. I went into my room and read a Hardy Boys for a while, then turned out the light. I was hoping that I would have more of those interesting dreams I'd had in the coffin. But I didn't. I slept lightly, peacefully, dreamlessly.

Until about six o'clock in the morning.

Then I was awakened abruptly again by the sound of someone yelling. This time it was a piercing shriek, a real true bloodcurdler, and it took a moment for me to realize that it was my mother who had screamed, out in the kitchen. I slipped into my pants and ran shoeless, shirtless, to the noise.

My father had just got there before me, rumpled and unbuttoned. "What in the world?" he asked.

She couldn't speak. She leaned white-faced against the doorway of the alcove and pointed a trembling finger.

There, sitting in the open icebox on a plate garnished with lettuce, was a skull. Two chrysanthemums glowed red in its eye sockets. A dead corn snake dangled out of its pearly teeth.

My mother cowered in my father's embrace. "I was just getting milk for our *oatmeal*," she said.

"I can see how it would give you a turn," he said. "I wonder what he did with the rest of it?"

We came to find out that Uncle Runkin had dismantled the skeleton and hid the pieces everywhere around the house. When you went looking for a Mason jar rubber or a length of string you would turn up a toe bone or a metacarpal. There are 206 bones in the adult human body and Uncle Runkin found 3,034 hiding places for them. Just the other day—twenty years afterward—I found in an old tackle box a kneecap. It brought back tender memories.

Eight / *Satan Says*

There came a time when Doc McGreavy had grown too
old to ride his horse, and I was glad because I was frightened of that horse. He was fitly named Satan, a glossy
black stallion, black as oil in the bottom of a barrel, and
stood, I would now guess, maybe sixteen hands high. It
seemed to me that in the late afternoon he cast a shadow
darker than other shadows. His nature was testy; he
rolled his eyes fiercely and curled his lip back from the
bit when Doc McGreavy rode him past our house, going
out on a call or returning to his home at the very end of
the road under Ember Mountain.

Kids will sometimes seize upon something to be frightened of. A boy willing to stand up to the roughest bully
in the school yard may be terrified that a hen will peck
his hands. Girls will sometimes choose an uncle to hide
from when he comes to visit, peeping at him from behind doorjambs and sofas. They choose these fears and
cannot say why, but there is a secret delight in them.

I was as frightened of Doc McGreavy as I was of Satan,
and one large part of my fright is understandable. Mc-
Greavy was what we called a "horse doctor"—that is,
someone without formal training who practices veterinary medicine—and he had been associated in my mind

from an early age with the blood and sickness and terror of our animals, with their guttural moans and surprising high-pitched screams. He was probably no worse than scores of other horse doctors in the Carolina mountains, but I never grew accustomed to his savage abrupt handling of animals as he yanked their mouths open or shouldered them over into the straw.

Even the tools of his trade suggested cruelty, the long-handled castration clamps, the large-toothed stubby saw for dehorning steers, the enormous forceps and hypodermics. The medicines in large brown and blue bottles were disgusting as well as threatening, and the words *nux vomica* suggested ugly sorceries. When I wanted to give myself a bit of a thrill before going to sleep, I would lie on my back and peer up into the dark and whisper, "Nux vomica, nux . . . vom-ica."

Johnson Gibbs had little patience with my penchant for scary fantasies. He considered that I was lucky to have parents and even a grandmother to live with. I had a large number of uncles and aunts also, and Johnson regarded this state of affairs as unwarranted luxury. So when I confessed some of my wilder hopes and fears to him he would say, "You're going all mush-headed, Jess. That's the kind of stuff a girl would say." The withering scorn with which he invested the syllable *girl* would silence me for a while.

Yet he largely shared my feelings about Doc McGreavy. Johnson was less afraid of the horse, but he was apprehensive of the man. And just as Satan was black, there was something dim and dark about his rider too. The doctor wore a black waistcoat with oversized sleeves and his black felt hat with its shapeless crown and wide brim was always pulled low over his brow. In the shade of the hat his eyes behind the tiny rimless spectacles glinted weirdly.

And in truth, his mind was given over to strange habits. He sang in a soft monotone as he rode along. We strained to distinguish the words but could make out few of them and, of course, I took pains to imagine that they were a litany of evil incantation. He seemed always to be preoccupied, never looking at the person who spoke to him, never turning his head toward unusual sounds, and always mumbling to himself; yet he was aware of everything that occurred. Once when he came to look at our Jersey cow he left his open bag against the inner wall of a stall and I crept over to inspect it. He was talking to my father outside the barn door—there was no way he could see me—but just as I bent over to look in, he said, "Boy, leave that satchel alone. There's things in there ain't good for you." He had a dry crackling voice like the sound of leaves burning and I recoiled from the black valise as if I'd found a copperhead inside.

His worst habit—the one that Johnson and I most disliked and feared him for—was his abuse of our collie, Queenie, a cheerful and friendly dog who was indispensable in working the cattle. For whatever reason, for no reason at all, Doc McGreavy had conceived a bitter antipathy to Queenie and never missed an opportunity to lash at her with a stick or to heave a rock. These ministrations put Queenie quite out of temper, and there was bad blood on both sides. When she heard Satan's hooves ring in the gravel, Queenie would hide behind the boxwood at the edge of our yard, tensely hugging the ground, and when the great horse came by she would rush out and nip at the silky fetlocks. Satan seemed hardly to notice, the disturbance caused only a small flutter in his stride, but Doc McGreavy would become enraged and his low singsong congealed to a chilling sentence. "I'll come some dark night and poison that bitch," he said.

When Queenie died in early September my father said it was just natural old age, but Johnson and I were unconvinced. We wept a little when we dug her grave under the spiky plum tree and agreed that her body was too stiff and contorted for her death to have been natural.

"He went and done it," Johnson said. "He's got all that poison and stuff in his black bag. I'm satisfied it was him."

My face and neck were burning. "I wish he'd swallowed it," I said. "I wish I could make him take the same stuff."

"Don't you worry," Johnson said. "His time's coming."

I don't know what Johnson intended by his vague threat, and I don't think he knew either. There was no way we could work any revenge on the old man; he was too powerful, allied with the forces of darkness, and we were feckless boys. That rankled, and made our fantasies all the more virulent.

"We could get some cockleburrs and put them under his saddle," I suggested.

"Pour a bushel of black widow spiders in his old satchel," Johnson countered.

"Grease that footlog over the creek to his springhouse so he'd fall in and drown."

"Steal his horse and hide him off in the woods somewhere."

But this final notion brought us to our senses. I was too scared of Satan to aid in that project.

We lowered Queenie into the crude rooty hole and shoveled her over as gently as we could. We stared at the mound for a while, then turned away. I think that we both wanted to say a prayer for her, but were too ashamed in front of each other.

We continued thinking of revenges but kept quiet about it because my father was friendly with Doc McGreavy. When Johnson muttered his aversion, my father said, "Now you want to go easy. The old man's a little addled in his head, but he's as good as any vet we've got around here. He's the only one that stays halfway sober."

"I don't like the way he treats them," Johnson said, "jerking them calves around and kicking them."

"He's not scientifically up-to-date," my father said. "He's what we've got. Shows you what kinds of opportunity there are. You could go to vet school, Johnson, and come back here to the mountains and do a world of good."

"Not me," Johnson said. "I wouldn't have that job for a zillion dollars. I can't stand to see them suffer."

"You have to get toughened up to it, not get personal."

"He's got too tough. How'd you like to have him operate on you?"

He looked at us with conscious patience. "He's a little crazy, that's all. I understand he's still got a Cuban bullet in him from the Spanish-American War. He doesn't mean any harm and I wish you boys would try to think better of him."

We said Yessir but we weren't going to. I thought Johnson had struck close to the source. When I watched Doc McGreavy dehorn a steer with that stubby saw I thought how it would be if he cut my arm off. Johnson would pin the steer against the side of the stall and my father and I twisted the head around until the eyes showed white and the mouth frothed and dripped over our hands and legs. It seemed to take forever. Or what if the doctor came at me with those castration clamps? When I thought of that the juices curdled in my stomach.

I asked Johnson about it when we lay in our separate beds in the dark bedroom. "You ever think about Doc McGreavy operating on you with those veterinary things?"

"No," he said quickly. "And I wish you hadn't thought of it right when I'm going to sleep."

"It's not long till Halloween," I said. "Think about that."

I heard him turn on his side. "I've been thinking," he said, "but I ain't made no headway. What you got in mind?"

"Nothing," I said. "Only that we ought to pay Doc McGreavy a visit."

He made an impolite noise of impatience. "I done took that for granted a long time ago. I thought maybe you had a bright idea."

"Do you?"

"No," he said, "but I pray to Jesus every night to help me think of some lowdown trick."

As Halloween drew closer Johnson and I listened with special attention to my father's supper table reminiscences, which were about all the lowdown tricks he'd heard of when he was a kid. We were particularly inter-

ested in distinguishing the ones he'd heard about from
the ones he'd participated in. That wasn't hard. When he
began by saying, "I heard one time about some old mean
boys who—" and broke off, giggling until he had a cough-
ing fit, we knew that he'd been in on that one himself,
and that the memory was still sweet pleasure.

But the pranks he recounted were useless to us, either
dully unimaginative or much too complicated. Johnson
and I had agreed that we weren't going to be so dumb as
to stop up chimneys or push over outhouses, but neither
could we picture ourselves taking apart a model-A Ford
and reassembling it on a barn roof.

"Your daddy didn't start out very promising," Johnson
said, "but he sure has got better over the years."

One hint stuck with us. "The best kind of trick," my
father said, "is one that actually does scare somebody.
That's what Halloween is all about."

"And one that doesn't do anybody any harm," my
mother put in.

"Oh yes, right," he said hastily. "One that doesn't do
any harm."

So Johnson and I were thrown back on our own mental
resources and discovered that they were not so powerful
as we had imagined. Scarecrows, witches with bubbling
cauldrons, goblins, whining ghosts—it was all too much
like the paper cutout display the teacher had pinned up
in the schoolroom, not an ounce of scare in a ton of it.

"What do you think a ghost would look like?" Johnson asked me.

"White, I reckon, and kind of fluttery and goes Wooo."

He shook his head morosely. "Can't you do no better
than that?"

"Make it purple," I said, and then with sudden inspiration, "No, make it red. Blood all over it."

"Blood coming out of its mouth," Johnson said.

"Blood leaking out of its nasty eyes," I said.

"Now we're getting somewhere. Who do you think it's
the ghost of?"

"Napoleon," I said.

"Napoleon?" He gave me a look of fathomless disgust. "Pack rats have carried off your brains, Jess."

"Well, who then?"

"Didn't we hear tell his wife died a few years back? I bet he wasn't nothing but awful to her. I bet she'd come back to haunt him if she could stand the sight of the old bastard."

"How'd we make a ghost of her? We don't know what she looked like."

"Just as long as it's a female ghost," Johnson said. "He'd get the idea in a jiffy."

"Put her in a nightgown."

"And get a wig," Johnson said, "long white scary hair and blood coming all out of her. She pops up at the bedroom window. *Hooo. McGreavy, you done me awful. I have come back to haunt you forever.*"

"*I will never give you any peace,*" I put in.

"*At your final hour I will await you beyond the Gate,*" Johnson intoned.

"Wonder what her name was," I said. "We need to know that."

My mother told me her name was Esther and that she was the dearest prize in creation. "She was so delightful. Always cheerful and smiling, and the soul of patience. When I was a little girl I used to look at her and think how pretty she was and hope to look like her when I grew up." She went on to tell how Mrs. McGreavy had died of tuberculosis, and how her death had affected the doctor. "That's when he began behaving so queerly," she said. "It must have been just awful for him."

But the sad story didn't move us. We had set our hearts stony.

"Esther," Johnson said. "*Hooo. Don't your recognize your Esther, come back from the grave!*"

The construction of the ghost presented some difficulties. Johnson collected the blood from the beheading of a Sunday dinner chicken and daubed it over some discarded glass curtains from the attic, but it didn't make a very striking color, turning a dull brown where it dried

in the cloth. The best color we found was a shade of fingernail polish called Passion Fire and we bought sixteen
bottles of it at Virgil Campbell's grocery. Mr. Campbell
regarded us curiously. "You boys will surely be the belles
of the ball," he said, and Johnson told him we were using
it to paint model airplanes.

The wig, though, was quite successful. Johnson had
taken a double handful of seagrass twine, knotted it intricately together, and combed out the strands. Squint
your eyes and it did look like the hair of a woman three
years dead, if that's the kind of image you were thinking
of every waking moment.

We'd rigged up two sticks in cruciform and popped an
acorn squash on for a head and draped three layers of
glass curtain over it all and streaked it good with nail
polish. Johnson took a smoldering stick and burned two
eyes and a nose-hole and we liberally bathed the edges of
these with polish. We pinned the wig on.

But when we inserted it into a mound of hay in the
barn loft and stood back to admire our night-gaunt, I was
disappointed. It looked exactly like ratty old glass curtains spattered with fingernail polish and sporting a
hank of seagrass twine.

Johnson noticed I was crestfallen and said, "You ain't
giving it a proper chance. Of course it don't look like
shucks up here in the barn loft in broad daylight. But
you see it come oozing up at your window on a dark Halloween night and hear its ghostally moans, you'd have a
different feeling about it. Especially if you was a crazy
old man that hadn't done nothing but meanousness all
your life."

"I hope you're right," I sighed.

"Sure I'm right," he said. "You think I don't know how
to scare people?"

That was two days before, and by the time Halloween
arrived I'd come around to Johnson's view. In fact, I was
in such a fever to get started that Johnson wrestled me to
the ground and sat on me. "When are you going to learn

some patience?" he asked. "You'll get too anxious and spoil the whole thing."

"Lemme up," I panted. "I have learned some patience."

We were sure that my father would tell stories at the supper table, ghost stories or tales of Halloween pranks, but he was silent. He stared at us with gravely speculative eyes and finally asked what we were going to be up to. "I don't want to hear of you doing anything that would hurt somebody or damage any property," he said. "Are we clear on that?"

"Yes sir," Johnson said. "We wouldn't do nothing bad."

"Jess?"

I told him Yessir, squirming in my clothes. It was already dark outside and Johnson hadn't made the first move to leave the table.

"Another thing," he said. "I've had a hard day and I need my sleep. If you boys come back one minute after ten o'clock I don't want to know about it. I don't want to see the lights on and hear a lot of clattering around."

"Yes sir," Johnson said. "We'll be as quiet—as quiet as a mouse." I knew he had started to say, *quiet as a rat pissing on cotton.*

"Quiet as a mouse is fine," he said. "And dark as a bat too. You hear?"

"Yes sir."

At last we left the table and went outside. It was a storybook Halloween night, calm and clear and breezeless. Scattered house lights were orange dots in the distance and now and then a dog would start up barking and then fall silent. Isolated stars shone in the east, but in the west they were washed out as the full moon nestled grandly on the hill ridges, a wheel of frost. In the moonlight Johnson looked taller and I moved a little closer to him in the road.

"Did you have to wear them corduroy pants?" he said. "Anybody can hear you coming half a mile off."

We went into the barn and collected our ghost. Johnson carried the squash and the vestments and I balanced the crossed sticks over my shoulder and we set off along the road again. It was finely thrilling, with the moon silvering hill and tree and stone, the mountaintops notching the blue-black horizon, the occasional scurry of some little animal in the weeds. The sound of our marching through the gravel was a steady comfort.

These details began to work upon me and I thought that now I was experiencing the real true nighttime of the world and I began to wonder how anyone ever dared go out into it. There were things present in the world that people must have agreed never to think about, things that demanded meditation and propitiation. It was a good two miles to Doc McGreavy's house and I had plenty of time for out of the way thoughts. The fence posts went by one by one and the lichen splotches on them looked like silver flowers from the planet Uranus.

Then Johnson halted and looked ahead. We were coming to the end of the road, where the powerlines stopped— Doc McGreavy had not cared to install electricity—and huge-armed oaks made the avenue a cavern of slatted darkness. "We'll get off here," Johnson said, "and go down through the pasture so he won't hear us coming."

We crossed the fence and the pasture grass was cold and wet. We couldn't see McGreavy's house, which was some two hundred yards beyond the edge of the shadow, but Johnson ducked his head, hunched his shoulders, and went forward on the balls of his feet. This was his way, as he had told me, of moving like a wolf.

I had expected to see a house light when we got into the shadow, but it took a while to make it out. The tree shadow went over us like a ruined roof and there was nothing before us but bars of moonlight through the dense bare limbs. Then we could see the dim weathered shape of the old house and a diffuse yellow-orange glow at the back.

"He's back in the kitchen," Johnson whispered. "That's good."

It was very good indeed. He had said earlier that to prevent discovery we would crawl the last five hundred yards the way soldiers and Indians did. That sounded good at the time, but we hadn't counted on such daunting cold ground.

So we sneaked up in an awkward half-crouch. I'd seen this house countless times but it made a different impression upon me now, gray and streaked with shadow, tall and peaked and forlorn. I'd like to think that we moved soundlessly from shadow to shadow to the back of the house. But I kept snagging the cross framework in bushes and knocking myself in the jaw when I tore it free, and the folds of curtain dripped from Johnson's hands and he kept crushing them into the grass and swearing.

Finally though we arrived at the kitchen window, Johnson on one side and I on the other. He gave me a slow solemn nod and we stretched up to look inside.

It was a large room but it looked small and cozy in the glow of the kerosene lamp which sat on the table oilcloth. The big wood range took up a lot of space and the huge black shape of Satan took up even more. Doc Mc-Greavy was turned away from us, stirring in a big pot on the stove, not even glancing back at the horse. We could hear his singsong mumble keep time to his stirring. There were two large soup bowls on the table and he brought the pot from the stove and ladled them full. Steam rose pale orange in the lamplight.

He set the pot back and jammed a lid on it. "There now, Satan," he said. "There's our supper."

The great horse brought his nose carefully over the table. When the steam touched his nostrils he jerked his head back suddenly and his liquid eyes rolled and gleamed yellow. He pawed the floor once and with my shoulder against the wall I could feel the shudder of it through the whole house.

"Too hot for you?" Doc McGreavy asked. "Just wait a minute and it'll cool down." He turned the damper on the stovepipe and went to the wall cabinet and got a cup and poured himself coffee from the pot at the back of the range. He opened the warmer and took out four doughy biscuits and set them on the checked oilcloth. He pulled out a straight chair and sat. "Eat you a biscuit while we're waiting for the soup to cool."

Satan curled his lips and took up a biscuit as daintily as a society dame accepts a petit four. Then he chewed it and crumbs sprayed everywhere.

McGreavy propped his elbows on the table and sipped at his coffee. "Seems to me, Satan, that you get blacker with every day that goes by."

The horse gave a curt awkward nod.

"If you get any blacker I'm going to paint white spots on you so folks can see you coming at night."

Satan snorted softly.

Doc McGreavy picked up a big tin spoon and tested the soup. He nodded. "It's cool enough now. Go ahead and try it. I've got a little storebought cake for later."

Satan nosed carefully to the bowl and then drew slowly back and shook his head.

"What's the matter? . . . You say there's not enough marrow in it? Why, Satan, there's plenty of good marrow in this soup. Half a beef shinbone."

But the horse hung away from the table, switched his broomy tail.

"Not enough blood and bones in this soup? Now that's silly. What kind of blood and bones do you want?"

He pawed the floor three times.

"Human blood?" Doc McGreavy asked. "Surely to God you don't want no human blood in our soup. Where would I get any human blood?"

He gave a quick toss of his head, and the way the lamplight caught his eye made it look as if there were a fire inside his skull. His mane gleamed.

"What's that? You say there's some lowdown boys looking in our little window?" McGreavy turned his head toward us and the light flashed across his tiny spectacles like moon-glint on knifeblades. "Who do you reckon they are?"

Then Satan spoke. There was never a voice like that in the world. It was deep and dark and full of power like a

146

boulder tearing open. There were abandoned wells in that voice and haunted caves and rotten graves opening from inside. I was hot and cold and sweaty and the hair on my neck and forearms rose stiff as quills. "Let's invite them in for supper," Satan said.

Until this moment I had been too scared to run, but Satan's cordial invitation fortified my courage and I threw down those stupid sticks and lit out like a rabbit that feels the panting of the hounds. I ran heedless through muddy ditches, briars and thorn bushes and, for all I know, straight through the barbwire fence. I certainly do not remember stopping to climb across it.

I ran down the gravel road till I was out of breath and could run no more. My clothes were shredded and I was sweating and bleeding and gasping, doing everything but breathing sanely. I felt too naked and easy to get at in the road and went to the edge and squatted down in some sassafras bushes, waiting till I got my wind back so I could run another mile or five or ten miles.

I heard someone walking toward me in the road and I prayed it was Johnson Gibbs. I knew I wasn't going to move until I saw every feature of his face. I recognized his voice when he called out, "Jess? Jess, where you at?" And still I wouldn't move.

When he was close enough to reach out and touch, I said quietly, "Here I am, Johnson."

"What are you doing in the bushes?" he asked.

"Hiding to save my life," I said.

"What are you talking about? Why didn't you pass me them sticks so I could rig up and scare the old man?"

"Are you crazy? After Satan offered to eat us up?"

"Offered to what?"

"Didn't you hear him talk?"

"No I never. What did he say?"

"He said, Let's eat their brains and bones."

"You sure about that? You sure he didn't say something different?" Johnson's voice dropped in pitch and sounded deep and hollow. *Let's invite them in for supper.*

That was the voice, all right, and I flew at him and pounded his chest with my fists. He didn't protect himself, he was laughing too hard for that. I punched him until I was exhausted, but he was too happy to feel a single blow.

"That wasn't fair the way you-all tricked me," I said, "not a bit fair. You and me was supposed to be in this together. It was our Halloween rusty, yours and mine."

His laughter had subsided to giggles. "Let me tell you about how we done it," he said.

"No," I said. "Just hush up. I don't want to hear a word out of you."

We walked along toward the house. He was still chuckling and I was still enraged. "Just let me tell you—"

"Shut up!" I shouted. "I done told you to just shut up."

"Now, Jess," he said, but he went quiet until we came into the shadow of our house. Then he said quietly, "One thing, though. Doc McGreavy didn't poison Queenie. We were all wrong about that."

"Hush up, Johnson," I said wearily, and he giggled again.

"I wish I could stop laughing," he said. "My ribs hurt where you come punching on me."

The house was dark and silent and we remembered my father's warning to keep quiet when we came in. We entered through the sun parlor and got through that and the hallway all right—though I thought that my harsh breathing was loud enough to wake the household—and felt in the darkness and began to climb the steps. We had got halfway up when a gray-white apparition suddenly appeared at the top and flapped itself at us.

"Doom, doom!" the gray ghost cried. "Doom to all who disturb the peace of the night."

"Oh Lord, Jess," Johnson said. "You had better hold my hand. I'm so scared I must be going to have a heart attack. How will we ever endure this awful fright?"

He struck a match and in its glow we saw my father lift the folds of the sheet and peer out from under, pleased and vexed at once, like a cat interrupted at the cream

148

pitcher. He shook his head petulantly. "Well, you ought to have been scared," he said. "If you had any imagination you would be. That's the trouble with Halloween these days. Nobody's got any imagination."

I felt a twinge of pity for him and said, "I was scared."

He brightened. "Were you, Jess?"

"Sure, I was scared. A little bit."

"Well, but you scare pretty easy, don't you?" Johnson said.

I hit him again, trying to find the tenderest rib.

Nine / *The Wish*

Sleep, that lurid bottomless ocean. I came up out of it in slow confusion, a diver struggling back to the surface of the world. When I opened my eyes, a pale blurred beacon hung in darkness before me, the broad face of my father.

"Wake up, Jess," he was saying in low tones. "Time to wake up if we're going to get gone."

"What time is it?" The words came out of my mouth gummy and reluctant.

"Time to leave," he said. "I've already got our stuff together. You be quiet now and don't wake up your mother and grandmother. I'll wait for you down in the kitchen." The dim lantern of his face went away and I heard him move softly out of the room, leaving the door open.

I sat up and swung my legs over. I almost spoke to the bed across from mine, to say, *Johnson, wake up, time to go,* but then realized, as sleep washed out of me, that the bed was empty, abandoned forever.

To go fishing with your father: that is an ancient and elemental proposition, and if it is not as overwhelming as sex or death or the secret lives of animals, still there are legendary shadows about it entrancing to a boy twelve years old. And this would be the first time in a long time that my father and I had been much alone together.

I dressed as quietly and efficiently as I could in this dark upstairs bedroom but of course got my cotton sweater on backward and had to squirm it around. I carried my socks and heavy brogans so that I wouldn't blunder noisily on the stairs and then sneaked out and down to the kitchen. I was dead certain that I moved as silently as dandelion fluff and could not have disturbed the sleep of an otter.

My mother was awake, though, and sat at the table with my father as he sipped noisily at a steaming cup. "Good morning, Jess," she said cheerily. "You're awake bright and early this morning."

I blinked at her in the bald white light.

"He doesn't look awake to me," my father said. "This is just some old sleepwalker wandering in."

"I'm awake," I said. The phrase came out as a squeaky yawn.

"Have some coffee," he said. "That'll get your motor turned over."

"Joe Robert, you're not going to give this child coffee," my mother said.

"Sure I am. I want my fishing partner alert and ready for action." He took down a chipped blue cup and poured into it a little coffee and a lot of milk. He set it by me on the table, where I leaned over in the chair dragging on my brogans. "See if that doesn't fix you up proper," he said.

Already this September Saturday was an important day, beginning as it did with my first cup of coffee in my life. I drank it slowly and disliked it thoroughly.

"Well, it's easy to see that you boys are feeling your oats," my mother said. "Just don't get carried away. You be careful out there on the lake."

"How do you like that coffee?" he asked.

"It's real real good," I said.

"All right then. You ready to hit the trail?"

"Sure."

"Don't wait up for us, honey," he said. "We might be gone a week. We might like it so much we'll decide to live out our lives in a boat."

"If you catch any fish," she said, "you be sure you clean them. They're ugly enough when they've been cleaned. If they're not cleaned I won't even look at them."

"You just don't know how to appreciate good fish," he said. They engaged in a kiss that wasn't brief enough to suit me as I stared at the wall. "Let's go, Jess," he said, and we went out and got into the car.

The back of the old Pontiac was full of fishing gear and the big wicker picnic basket. My father turned in the driver's seat and surveyed our stuff in the glow of the dashboard lights. "Whatever we've forgotten we'll just have to do without," he said and pushed the starter knob. We pulled away.

It was a cool morning and white dawn light made the east pallid. The trees were readying to turn, the beeches and oaks and locusts along the roadside, intimations of autumn. He seemed happier than he had been in many weeks. He glanced at me now and again as we rode along and winked at me, but the wink was sad. "Going to be a cool day," he said. "Did you put our jackets in like I told you?"

"Yessir."

We drove twenty-three miles on the asphalt road and then through the tall hills on a dirt road and then turned into a rutted pine-needle path down to the water.

The air by the lake was much cooler. I put on my green wool jacket, envying my father his big sheepskin in which he looked so cozy. We stood by the car for a moment, gazing out. From the edge of the water a long flimsy plankway led to the door of a rickety little shack which sat stilted over the lake. From the tiny tin chimney spiraled a thread of dark smoke, so that the building looked like a great water spider with a single unruly hair growing from its body. We trudged up the plankway, carefully sliding one foot before the other. When I looked down at the cold water, imagining falling in, gooseflesh came over me. My father knocked at the door.

A small old man opened the door and put his head out. He peeped at us without much show of friendliness.

"What are you fellers a-wantin'?" he asked.

"Good morning to you, sir," my father said. "We're hoping to rent a boat from you, figured we might do a little fishing."

"Want you a boat, eh?" He craned his head around the edge of the doorway and spat a dollop of tobacco juice into the water, and as he moved forward I saw that he was a hunchback. I wasn't surprised; it seemed in keeping with his demeanor. He held the door open. "Well, come on in, then," he said.

We went in and looked about the single primitive room. The thrumming wood heater in the middle drew us and we put our hands toward it palm up, siphoning in its good heat.

The little old man stood beside us, looking us up and down. He was trying to figure us out. "Don't know how much fishing you fellers'll get done today," he said. "It looks to me like we're going to get a little rain."

"Then we'll just have to come on back in," my father said. "We've been planning this a long time. Seems like we don't get many chances to go fishing." He shook hands with the old man and introduced himself and then placed his hand on my head. "And this is my boy, Jess," he said.

The old man nodded and offered me his hand. It felt as hard and raw as rusty iron.

"How-do," he said. "My name's John Clinchley, but they've always called me Sack. I don't know how that come about." His voice was low and raspy, sounded like rusty metal bending. The pupils of his eyes were dark brown, the whites yellowish. His body was bunched forward and he stared up at my father like someone peering out of a cave. He rubbed his nose with his thumb knuckle. "Well, I reckon I got a boat for you if you want to go out," he said. "Might be you can get in some pretty fair fishing before the rain commences. Can't never tell."

My father settled with him the details about renting the boat, and then we went out and transferred our tackle and the food into it. We clambered in, trying not to get wet, and I shoved us off with one of the heavy handmade paddles. The motor caught on the fourth try and my father maneuvered the boat out toward the long, low farther rim of the lake. I looked back and saw the old man standing on the sagging plankway, watching. I waved at him and he nodded, almost imperceptibly. The broad-bottomed boat was awkward, too large for the little outboard motor to push very fast.

We found a spot we liked, not far up the lake next to a likely looking shelf of rock, but the water was too deep; the anchor chain wasn't long enough. The boat floor was scabbed with damp mud and three empty bait cans rolled about under our feet. I finally filled them with water and let them drift down to lake bottom. We came to another place we liked, quite shallow, reedy, with methane bubbles rising now and then to the surface. The lake ran deep on both sides here, and it looked inviting, if not promising.

My father tied on a three-piece plug, red with black pop-eyes, and held it up for inspection. I grinned. The lure looked like a space monster from the Buck Rogers comic strip. But he had trouble casting; the first attempt landed only about six feet from the boat. "I've been away from it too long," he said. At last the rhythm returned and he got longer and more accurate casts. "There," he said. "That's better."

"It would just about have to be better," I said.

"Let me tell you, Jess: nobody likes a smart-mouth kid."

We fished there for a long while with no luck. We moved farther up the lake against a steep clay bank. My father changed lures four times but didn't get the least hint of a strike. In an hour or so he pulled his plug in. I had already given up drowning redworms and was just lying lazy against the smooth motor housing. He reached for the food and made a couple of sandwiches and handed one to me; looked at the sky. It must have been about ten o'clock.

"Somebody told these fish we were coming," he said.

I chewed my pork chop sandwich. "Uh-huh."

"Look here," he said, "I found a bottle of wine Uncle Luden left behind. You ever had any wine?"

"No sir."

He opened the corkscrew of his pocket knife and worried the cork out. "You can have some of this if you don't tell your mama."

I took the tin cup and tasted it, red and sour. "It's real good," I said, silently cataloging it with coffee as nasty stuff, nothing like the wine I remembered with Uncle Luden on the mountaintop.

"Think there's any fish in this lake?" The sun had got warmer and the breeze had died. He took off his sheepskin and made a pillow against the gunwale, leaned back to eat and sip.

"I don't know."

We munched and pondered. My father smoked a cigarette.

"We'll get some fish," he said. He burned the line above the lure in two with his cigarette and bit three small sinkers onto the line, grimacing as the lead thrilled his teeth. From the tackle box he took a number two barbed hook, kneaded a lump of the sandwich bread over it and dropped it into the water, not too deep. He waggled the tip of the rod and then drew it slowly like a wand back and forth along the side of the boat. After a few minutes he jerked the rod sharply and pulled up a spiny bream. He took it carefully off the hook—cautious with the spines—and knocked it dead on the edge of the boat. He made more bread balls and caught four more little bream.

We pushed the food to one side and left this spot and went farther again up the lake. There was another boat at a rocky point over to the right and we gave it a wide margin, pushing straight up the main channel. We had the throttle full out, but the boat didn't move very fast. Slapping and then sucking back like a rubber glove pulled off, the water beat against the side of the boat. A wide swath trailed behind, flat and smooth for a moment, then curling inward, closing over, lacy, a long acute triangle devouring itself. We got out of sight of the other boat and went up into a narrow inlet with scrubby pines growing above the parallel long, sandy banks. Cut the motor. Over the side with the anchor, two window-sash weights wired together. My father took up one of the little fish he had caught and began to gouge out its eye with his knife.

"Ough," I said. "Gah. What makes you want to do that?"

"You want to catch some fish, don't you?"

"Ugh. I don't know."

"Don't go squeamish on me, Jess." He took an empty penny matchbox and dropped nine eyes into it. One of them he had squashed to pulp in trying to dislodge it. The eyeless fish had idiot faces; he threw them up on the sand. He tied on a larger hook and fitted one of the eyes precisely over the barb and then cast forward in an arc parallel to the bank. I watched the whole process rather uneasily.

On the third cast he got a pretty hefty strike. He set the hook quickly and began to reel in. The fish flashed in the air, flecked the tense light with heavy spray. It fell to the water, the bright instant was gone. A nice bass. He let it play for a little while, then reeled it to boat side and scooped it in with the net. A nice smallmouth with a stupefied air and the hook far down his throat, almost in his belly. It took a long time to get the hook out and he mumbled that it was a size too large. The fish measured just over a foot.

"There you go," he said. "Now we know there's some in here."

I had already begun to tie on a hook. "Let me try one of those," I said.

He grinned and handed me the matchbox. "Doesn't it make you feel bad, using these fish eyes?"

I squinted to impale the eye on the hook. "Makes me feel good," I said. "I feel real good."

In a half hour or so we had caught six more fish. I was a bit frustrated, having lost two good strikes from anxiety. But I wasn't disappointed; all the fish were about the same size as the first.

Then we were out of bait.

"Why don't we pull over to the bank and catch some more bream?" I asked.

"Maybe we don't need to," my father said. "Maybe they've remembered how to bite by now, maybe we've taught them the right idea." He got rid of the bare hook and tied on the little Martian plug. I watched him intently for a few minutes, then turned to the picnic basket and got out a chicken leg. It must have been nearly noon.

"We forgot to bring any cheese," I said.

"Shoo, old cheese," he said. "Makes you constipated."

He looped an easy cast about thirty feet out toward the main current and began reeling in. He hesitated for a moment, as if his line had snagged, and then jerked the rod viciously, setting the hook. An instantaneous rainbow off to the left of the boat: a large fish gathered itself and tried to shake free. My father reeled quickly and the line got taut and steady, heavy, tense. On the wrinkled plane of the lake the imaged sun was a marigold, slashed through continually by the tight blue-green line. He played with the fish about three minutes before bringing it in and killing it. A good fish, about eighteen inches long.

"That's a dandy," I said.

"You think we ought to keep this one or throw him back?"

"He's dead, you can't throw him back. He's a jim-dandy."

He dabbled his hands in the lake and wiped them down the front of his blue cotton shirt. He took a chicken wing from the hamper and gnawed, sipped from the bottle. "You want some more wine?"

"No thank you," I said. "I'm already drinking this ice tea." Two gulps of that wine had been plenty and more than plenty.

He drew up the anchor and paddled toward the sandy

shore, using one of the rough oars. He beached the boat, pinned the oar handle two feet into the sand and wrapped the anchor chain about it. I finished the chicken leg and tossed the bone into the water, climbed out of the boat and stood unsteadily.

My father was gathering dry driftwood and had soon started a fire. Then he went back to the boat and began gutting the fish. "This is your mother's strict orders," he said. With awkward nervous strokes he slit underneath from the back toward the gills, scraping at the insides and cutting at the muscle and horny skin at the throat. "Here's Mama Bear," he said. "Now we'll stop calling this big 'un *he*." He showed me the long frothy row of eggs.

"Throw them in the water," I said. "Maybe they'll hatch."

"They will if you'll set on them," he said.

He slipped a length of cord through the mouths and gills and let the fish wash in the water, attached to a ring on the prow of the boat. He went back and gathered more firewood and sat by the flimsy blaze, smoking a cigarette, breathing the smoke deeply. "Jess," he called, "fetch me my jacket and the rest of that bottle." I brought them along and he made a pillow of the sheepskin and lay propped on his side, sipping and smoking. The white sun was woozy.

It had got cold and the breeze had sprung up again and the bitter edge of it woke me. The sun was hidden by a long opaque gray smear of cloud so that I couldn't tell the time, but I guessed it was about four o'clock. My father lay napping in the big woolly sheepskin. The fire was ashes and twig-ends. I walked up and down the scurfy sand, looking at the weather, looking north where the darkening cloud bank curved and gathered into a rolling sky-prairie of goose down. Then I went to my father and tugged at his elbow. "It's getting pretty dark," I said.

He stood up and surveyed the sky. "We'd better go on back." He kicked sand over the dead ashes.

"It's cold," I said.

We got into the boat and went out into the main channel. He looked up and down the lake, as if uncertain which way to turn.

We went southwest under the blackening sky. The clumsy boat made sloppy headway against the rising swell the breeze had pulled up. Across the water came the cold smell of moss and piny darkness. We went down a long way.

"Wait a minute," I said. "I think we missed the place right back there."

He turned and headed us into it, but it was only a shoebox-shaped notch of sheared rock, and we came out again.

"We'll keep close to the bank going down," my father said. "We can see to the end of most of these little coves."

"We'd better find it pretty soon," I said.

At the north end of the lake we heard the rain beginning, a sound like newspapers flapping open. "I wish we'd brought our raincoats," I said.

"Distress flares, that's what we need," he said.

The rain was on us now, icy, and making a gray lather of the lake surface. The current seemed stronger, the wavelets coming by less high. "Hey," I said, "we must be getting near the dam." I could hardly hear it over the gray rattling of the rain, but it was there, a solid steady booming like the sound of trees toppling. We turned and went back, keeping close to the right edge.

"We must have come down too far," my father said.

We were drenched and shivering and the damp mud in the boat had turned to slime. It was the miserablest condition I ever saw my father in, but the sight gave me no satisfaction at that moment. The rain hissed, sizzled on the hot motor. We kept brushing water out of our eyes.

At last we found the right place and brought the boat in and made fast. My father grabbed the tackle box and I carried the rods and the fish. The rest of the stuff we left. We ran up the plankway into the little stilted shack.

Immediately we felt suffocated and hot, and we dropped the gear and flung off our jackets. We stood around the marvelous amber-spattered stove where the little hunchbacked man was standing. In the light of the wheezing Coleman suspended from the overhead joist his eyes looked dimmer and yellower than they had this morning. He stood with his hands folded in front of him.

"I told you-all fellers we might get a speck or two of rain," he said.

"You were dead-on right," my father said.

"What time is it?" I asked.

He pulled a turnip watch from the bib of his overalls and flicked it open. "Twenty-five after."

"Four?"

"Five." He replaced the watch with a careless easy gesture.

The rain banged the roof and the north wall. The old man gazed at us as we shivered, and then, as if he had made a sudden decision, turned quickly and went to rummage in a pile of burlap sacks heaped against the wall. He returned to the stove bearing a quart jar half-filled with what looked like water. "Here," he said. "Might take the frost out of your bones a little."

My father looked at it. "Now what in the world might this be?" he asked.

For answer the old man unscrewed the top and took a long swallow and passed it to him. There was a thick brown smear where he had drunk. My father held the jar against the lantern light, peered through it. "Here's wishing you good health," he said, and drank. He turned to me. "You can't have any of this. Your mother wouldn't leave me an inch of hide."

"That's okay," I said, "I'm all right." I was pretty sure it would taste as bad as wine and coffee.

He took another sip and grinned and shivered, handed it back to the old man. "Not bad at all," he said.

"It's pretty good, as I judge," the old man said, and took another durable swallow. "Of course now, I don't know who made it and I ain't got no notion how it come to be here in the cabin." He passed it to my father again.

"Some fishermen passing through must have forgot and left it here," he said. He took a nip and said "Thank you" and returned it.

The old man took a final sip and screwed the top on and set the jar on a rickety shelf away from the stove.

"How long do you think it'll keep on?" my father asked.

The old man scratched a tuft of white hair in his left ear, hitched a gallus. "You can't never tell. Won't rain hard no long time, might spit a little two-three days."

"I'm hungry," I said.

"That's too bad, Jess," my father said. "Our food is out there dissolving in the rain."

"Ain't nothing in here but some store bread and a tub of lard," the old man said.

"We got fish," I said.

"Sure, that's right," my father said. "We caught a few."

We started to work. The old man took the eight fish to a corner and began hacking at them with a saw-edged knife. My father took the lid off the lard tub. The stuff was a filthy gray. With his pocket knife we peeled away the surface until he got a fairly white patch and then cut squares from it and laid them in the inverted tub lid. The old man brought the fish, cleanly scaled in almost no time. My father looked at them. "Let's hang them out in the rain a few minutes," he said. "It's coming down hard enough to wash them off." I took the slices of loaf bread off the stove where they had been left to scorch and harden. I snatched them off bare handed and dropped them into a paper bag and pounded the bag with my fist. My father refueled the stove with wood and set the tub lid with the lard squares in it on top, that was our frying pan. We brought the fish in out of the rain and stuffed them into the bag with the bread crumbs and shook it vigorously. On the stove the lard popped and sputtered and we put in the fish. The frizzly sound of frying filled

the shack and smelled strange and greasy and wonderful.
Then we took our time whittling little wooden gigs to
get the fish out with.

Eating, we didn't talk much. My father and the old
man drank whiskey with the meal, but I had to be
content with rainwater dipped from a bucket outside. I
didn't mind.

"How are you doing, Jess?" my father asked. "Still
hungry?"

"Fine," I said. "I sure ain't hungry."

The old man squinted at me. The three of us were sitting cross-legged on the floor. My father and I leaned
back into the pile of scale-encrusted burlap. The lake
water leaped and slapped beneath the floor and the rain
banged in random gusts; one wall of the shack was black
inside where the rain came through.

My father offered the old man a Camel and he took
it eagerly. "This here's the first factory-rolled I've had
in near two weeks," he said. With his tough thumb he
flicked the yellow paper tab of a tobacco bag which dangled from a pocket in the overalls bib. He struck a
kitchen match with his thumbnail and, as someone accustomed to homemade cigarettes, held the tube pinched
tightly with thumb and forefinger over the seam, in case
the spit hadn't glued it firm. "You're an educated feller,
ain't you?" he asked my father, omitting the *u* from
educated.

My father shrugged. "I've had schooling," he said. "I
don't know how much claim I'd lay to being educated."

"Yes," the old man said, "I knowed you was educated.
I can tell by the way a feller acts what kind of feller he is.
When you boys come in here this morning to get a boat,
why, you didn't act like no big shots, like you owned it
all. That's how I knowed. You take, it wasn't but a week
or so ago, a big-shot yankee kind of feller drove a big
fancy car down here—color of lic'rish it was—and set
out there and tooted his horn. I says to myself, Toot your
hind end off, I ain't going out there. He blowed it again,
oh four or five times, and I says to myself, Mister, if you're

craving a boat, you're going to have to walk up to the door and ask for it. I ain't your nigger nor nobody else's. Ended up, he finally marched on in. Lord, you never heard such high-horse talk. I just made out like I was hard of hearing. He says, Do you rent boats here? And I never let on. I says, I heard she was in the hospital up to Cedarville. Do you rent boats here? he says, and I says, I heard it was the female miseries, are you the man come to collect? He run red in the face like a beetroot. He said, You deef old fool. Talking softlike, you couldn't hardly hear him. Then he says, What's the matter, can't you hear?" The old man paused to give us a disconcerting wink and produced the serrated blade he had used earlier to clean the fish and held it easy in his hand. "I didn't say nothing at first. I just got this little old cleaning knife out and held it loose like this, and I says to him, Mister, I might be a deef old fool, but I'm going to make your wife a happy widder if you don't get out of here real quick. —He never said nothing. He just turned his back on me and stepped off. I says to myself, Why, that feller's just like me, he's ignorant, he don't know nothing. He's lucked up into some money somewhere along the line, but he wasn't no better than me when he started out. —See, that's how come I seen you was educated."

"There's different kinds of education," my father said. His voice sounded wise and melancholy, admiring.

But the old man didn't appear to hear him and went on talking.

Once, he said, he had farmed; had a good sixty-odd-acre place down in Avery County. Cotton, peanuts, tobacco, a little truck farming. His wife was a good woman, four younguns, but the children had all died before the eldest was ten years old. "I figure that's what done my old woman in at last," he said. "She was just wore out, grieving like that. Seemed like it hindered her mind some way." She was in the hospital three years. "The doctors done everything they could have thought of, but it didn't do no good." At the end she died; he had never seen anyone look so white. After that, he wasn't clear. It seemed to take every penny he could scrape up to pay the hospital and the doctors. "There wasn't nothing that looked like any use to me," he said. "I felt like I hadn't done nothing but grub out stumps them whole three years." He took to drinking then, drank whatever he could get his hands on. "It ruined me, the liquor did. But boys, I didn't know nothing. I kept thinking if they was a God in heaven, I wouldn't treat a yellow dog the way I'd been treated. Many a night I laid out in the fields in the rain that time." Finally he sold what was left of the farm; by then it had mostly gone to ragweed. His brother-in-law had got him his present job. "It ain't no job fitten for a man," he said, "but boys, I don't care. I ain't a man no more. I've been throwed away like a corn-shuck. I make my rations, is all I care about. I got me a shack up yonder in the woods about three hundred yards and it's a good tight roof, and that's all I care about." He spoke all this in a dreamy nostalgic voice warm with fondness, as if he had been recounting the biography of a close friend. It seemed that the old man liked the shape his life had made in his mind; it was like an antique statue of a goddess, beautiful in its ruined lineaments.

I looked at my father. He sat loose and still, his fore-arms lying like sticks of wood across his lap. He nodded once, gravely and slowly. The hard rain had stopped. We heard the wash of the lake and a light steady drizzle and the stillness of wet pines.

"We'd better be getting back," my father said. He rose stiffly.

It took a while to settle with the old man for the boat. He was reluctant to let us go and my father kept wanting to pay him more than he wanted to charge. "You boys come back now," he said. "It'll be better fishing when the days get a little cooler."

"All right," my father said. "We'll do that."

The rain had turned the lakeshore to mud, and the Pontiac was stuck. It took about fifteen minutes to get it moving, and we labored at it in silence, not looking at each other. Then the car was free.

We went back, and the road seemed shorter than it had when we went out in the morning. The old man had been right about the rain; it kept coming down in sticky spitlets which the wipers smeared on the windshield. The roadside houses and bushes looked bleary and small. We went down through the hills and through the lonesome river valley. Tipton was gray in the gray rain, no people about. We went up the dirt road and pulled into our driveway under the oak trees and sat in the car. There was warm yellow light in the windows of the kitchen, but we sat listening to the feathery drizzle on the car roof.

Then my father closed his eyes. He hit the steering wheel with the heel of his open hand four times. "Oh Jesus Jesus," he said. "I wish Johnson Gibbs hadn't got killed."

Ten / *Bright Star of a Summer Evening*

To the best of my knowledge, my grandmother made but one mild joke in her life and it went out over the radio.

It was broadcast on radio because she had accompanied Aunt Samantha Barefoot to the station for an interview. Aunt Sam was quite a famous person in our mountains, a prize fiddler and banjo player. She and my grandmother were cousins and had been close friends since they were children; so they must have been about the same age. Aunt Sam, though, looked much younger. Her terra-cotta hair was wild and frazzly, and two blue silk bows perched in it like butterflies on a tile roof. Her freckled face was scarcely wrinkled, her lively blue eyes shone with bright feeling and easy mischief. I got the impression that she was as full of mischief as my father, but that it was more acceptable in her because . . . Well, because whatever she did was acceptable.

Yet for all her mischief and adventurous talk and strange show business clothing, she was demure and straightforward. All the things that had happened to her in the many years of traveling her music had never touched her central innocence. Whatever she did and said was as natural to her as dignity to a cat, and beneath her noisy ways lay a deep reserve of dignity not a bit catlike.

When she came to stay with us for a while, she got out of her long sky-blue Cadillac wearing a calf-length denim cowgirl skirt and a red bandanna blouse and cowgirl boots, elaborately tooled. I made up my mind to take a slow tour of those boots when I got a chance. She tripped up the porch steps like a courting-age girl and wrapped my grandmother in a bosomy embrace. "Oh, look at you, Annie Barbara," she cried. "You haven't aged a minute in seven years. It makes me feel like something a possum has pissed on and buried."

My grandmother returned her hug and murmured endearments, her eyes closed.

Then she went round to each of us. My mother, she declared, looked like a movie star and had a fine reputation as a schoolteacher. She told my father that he would be mighty handsome if he wasn't so mean and trifling. She said it was grand that I read so many books, someday I would be a scholar of high renown. "Oh, it makes me so proud to see all of you that I'm just weeping," she said.

It was true. Tears welled from her blue eyes and streaked her freckled mannish face.

"Just let me get my Kleenex out of the car," she said, and tripped down the steps.

"For God's sake, don't let her get in the car," my father said. "She might drive off and leave us."

But she didn't. She searched in a huge leather bag and took out a handful of tissue and wiped her eyes and loudly, frankly, blew her nose. She came back to the porch, carrying the bag by its shoulder strap like a man fetching a bucket of water. "I'm going to sit down right here in a rocking chair," she said. "Seeing you-all look so fine has made me too excited."

We pulled the rocker up and she sat. Then we made a scurrying effort to find out if there was anything in the world she wanted: coffee, lemonade, tea, breakfast, dinner, or supper. If we had possessed a casket of jewels we would have poured them at her feet. I listened in amazement as my father offered to get a cushion.

"Joe Robert," she said, "my old ass is so tough I can't feel the good of a cushion."

Oh, I liked her immensely. She had already said out loud in front of everybody two words my mother didn't want me to think to myself in a closet. No one paid the slightest mind. I ran through the list of words I was forbidden to say—there must have been a dozen—and hoped she'd light on every one of them before she left. At the rate she was going, it wouldn't take ten minutes.

"Now tell us what-all you've been doing, Sam," my grandmother said.

"I came to find out about you," she said. "You don't want to hear about me."

"We don't?" my father said. "Well, why do you think we paid you to come?"

She giggled, and winked at my mother. "Didn't I say, *mean and trifling*? I bet he keeps you on your toes."

"I'm more interested in keeping her on her back," my father said.

That was a misplayed note and drew brief scalding glances from my mother and grandmother. But the remark delighted Aunt Sam and she laughed deeply and slapped her knees. Then she burst into tears again. "That would be just like what my Dundy might say," she said. "Lord, how I miss him." She dredged up another clutch of Kleenex and scoured her broad face.

I found out later from my father that Dundy had been her husband. He was a comic for the country music shows, prancing on stage in baggy plaid trousers and a famous beat-up hat. His opening line was, *The news is dismal in Limber Junction*, and his best routine was where he confused a veterinary who had delivered a foal with a doctor who was delivering his wife's first baby. He had begun in show business as an old-fashioned claw hammer banjo player and, when that style went out of fashion, had started telling the ancient cornball jokes country music fans liked to hear. ("Why didn't he tell new jokes?" I asked. —"If it's new, how would you know it was funny?" my father said. "Nobody's laughed at it yet.") It is the ordinary fate of comics to make everyone merry but themselves, and "Neighbor Dundy," as he was called, was a deeply sad man whose melancholy resulted in suicide.

This was but one of the misfortunes that darkened Aunt Sam's life. When she was seventeen years old and in the middle of her first road tour her father and mother and younger sister had perished in the fire that razed the old homestead in Cherokee County. Her youngest brother had lived on two years in agony before the mercy of his death. The older brother, formerly a brakeman, was paralyzed from a railroad accident. Her grandmother had died when Aunt Sam was a little girl, but her grandfather, at age seventy, had been shot in a boundary line dispute.

"And look how strong she's stood up under all that," my father said. "She knows how to live with her feelings. When she wants to cry, she just cries right in front of everybody and goes on with her business. When she wants to laugh, she doesn't hold back an inch."

Mostly she wanted to laugh and I noticed that after a day or so she began to hang close to my father, waiting for him to drop an observation or pull a rusty that would send her into purest gales. This was something of a strain on him because my father didn't think of himself as a funny man but rather as the earnest purveyor of unwelcome home truths. When his humor lost its sardonic edge, it was likely to become weakly silly. He was willing, however, to try to entertain Aunt Sam, and mostly failed. Then she realized what was happening and withdrew a little and was rewarded with the uncommon spectacle of my father's ordinary behavior.

Which now consisted in great part of trying to tease Aunt Sam into playing music for us on her fiddle or guitar or banjo. "I don't believe you've got it anymore," he said. "You've lost the touch. You've been deceiving those dumb hicks at the fairgrounds and the square dances."

She was adamant. "I made a solemn vow to myself," she said, "that I wouldn't play the first chord while I was here unless Cousin Annie Barbara joined in with me."

So then it was up to my grandmother and this was a startling revelation to me. "I didn't know she could play any music," I said.

"Oh but she can," Aunt Sam said. "When we were girls she could play circles around me."

"I didn't know that. I never heard her play nothing."

"She made a solemn vow too," Aunt Sam said. "A long time ago. But I wish you could have been there, Jess, a long time ago. She was so bright and handsome and talented in the music. I used to simply worship her. . . But of course you weren't thought of yet."

"He never was thought of," my father said. "He's just a by-product of the automotive age."

"Well, let's get her to play some, then," I said. "I want to hear it."

"You'll have a hard row uphill to persuade her," she said. "I've been trying for forty years and more."

"Why won't she play?"

"I'd better let her tell you. I'm not sure I understand it."

But she wouldn't tell me. My grandmother pursed her lips and shook her head. "It was a promise I made and I ain't to go back on it," she said.

"What kind of promise?"

"It was a personal promise," she said, and that's all she would say.

I had to go to my mother for enlightenment and she told me it was an old grudge my grandmother had always kept against her father. This was another hard revelation, that my grandmother had had a father. How was it possible for anyone ever to be older than she was? I had a sudden vision of my family lined up in a single file that stretched backward in time to Noah, each of them with an older and more Sorrells-like face. It was an image not inspiring in the least.

"Why was she mad at her daddy?" I asked.

"He stopped her from meeting the Queen of England," she said.

"How was she going to do that?"

"When she was fourteen she was already playing in the band for the best square dance troupe in the mountains. The dancers were invited to a festival in Scotland and they were to dance before the queen and then be presented to her. It meant a lot to Mama. It meant a lot to everybody, taking our music and dance across the ocean for the queen to enjoy. Her heart was just set on it. I've heard Aunt Minnie Lou tell about your grandmother practicing her curtsy in front of a mirror. For hours and hours."

"And her daddy wouldn't let her go?"

"Your great-grandfather Purgason was a stern old man with strict ideas," she said. "He was afraid that she'd spend the rest of her life in music and dancing."

"What's wrong with that?" I asked. I tried to picture my grandmother singing in front of audiences, dressed up like Aunt Sam and peppering her pious sentences with some nifty cuss words, but I soon gave up on that job, light years beyond the limits of my faculties.

"I don't know that there's anything wrong with it," my mother said. "But people had different notions in those days. My grandfather was old-timey religious. He thought the music and celebrity would be bad for your grandmother's character, that she would turn out to be a shallow and thoughtless person." She made a little squirrel-like noise of exasperation. "Can you imagine anybody thinking that about your grandmother?"

"No ma'am," I said, and I couldn't. In the recent hours my imagination had blown all its fuses. "Couldn't she go without his permission?"

"Oh, she'd never do that. She'd never do anything without her father's blessing. Aunt Samantha took her place in the band."

"Aunt Sam has met the Queen of England?"

"The way I heard it was that Mama swallowed her disappointment and took pains to coach Aunt Sam in the music, showed her how to play some of the difficult passages and so forth. You'd think there would have been bad feelings between the girls about it, but there never was." She paused to look out the kitchen window where a robin scavenged the circle of bare ground around the chopblock. "Don't you think your grandmother must have been a brave young girl?"

"What was she like, the Queen of England? What did she say?"

"You'll have to ask Aunt Samantha about that," my mother said.

"I'm going to," I said.

"Be sure and ask her when your grandmother is someplace else," she said.

But there was no need for that, as I learned from Aunt Sam. When she had returned from the festival in Scotland, she told my grandmother all about it many times in microscopic detail.

"What was she like, the Queen of England?"

"She was nice," she said, "an awful nice lady."

"How big was her crown?"

"She wasn't wearing a crown. She had on a white garden party hat with silk flowers and white gloves on her hands."

"How did people know she was the queen, if she wasn't wearing a crown?"

"Oh, it was easy to tell she was the queen," she said. "Nobody ever made a mistake about that."

"What did she say to you?"

"She said, *Thank you for coming.*"

"What else?"

"That was all she said."

"What did you say?"

"I didn't say anything. I just curtsied. Your grandmother showed me how to do that. We practiced it till my knees buckled."

172

"Didn't she invite you to come over to the palace for supper?"

Aunt Sam smiled. "No. I think maybe she wanted to and then it slipped her mind. There was a big crowd of us, it would have been a hard lot to feed."

"I'd like to meet her," I said. "I'd give anything to meet the Queen of England."

"Maybe you will someday," she said. "I hear she takes a keen interest in scholars of high renown. You keep on reading your books."

It seemed a plausible idea. The Queen of England had to be a busy person without much time to read. My plan would be to read the longest and most difficult book in the world, the book that nobody else ever read, and then go and tell her what was in it. She'd be glad to have that information.

"I guess you'll never forget about meeting the queen," I said.

"There's a lot of reasons I never will," she said.

These interrogations of the grownups had to take place over a period of four or five days because the house had become a restless and confusing place. Word had got abroad that Aunt Sam was visiting us and her local fame brought in a steady stream of visitors, more people than I'd seen in one place since my grandfather's funeral. And the telephone jingled incessantly, as if the tribe of Uncle Luden's girlfriends had rediscovered our number. No one seemed upset by all this confusion, not even my father. In fact, we took a fine pride because Aunt Sam had come to stay with us, as it was well known that she had many important friends in fancy places and could drop in for a visit on anyone she'd a mind to.

She showed a nice patience with all these people who were mostly strangers. Some of them she had known from years gone by and she greeted them with effusive warmth. Others laid claim to some tenuous obscure connection and she never denied them, though she didn't pretend to remember. "Law, honey," she would say, "I hope you'll forgive me, but I just can't recall. My old memory has got as weak as butterfly farts."

Of course, everyone asked her to play a good old tune or two, but she turned them down without hurting their feelings. If they persisted, she explained that she had made a personal promise having to do with her cousin Annie Barbara, and they had to be satisfied with that. It was obvious to anyone that Aunt Sam wasn't a deceiving person, she didn't waste her time trashing folks.

A lot of people came because they had heard her on the Grand Old Opry radio show which came out of Nashville, Tennessee. That was a show I'd never heard, the one radio program my grandmother forbade us to tune in. I'd never thought before why she wouldn't allow it, but now it was plain that the music stirred memories in her and fancies about what might have been and perhaps the old resentment toward her father. She wanted to keep her mind concentrated on running the farm and on Jesus, and, until Aunt Sam had showed up, she had quietly succeeded. Now, though, you might see her hanging back from the circle of admirers around her cousin, gazing with a mild but wistful speculation.

Who can fathom the motives of others? People in this world will do anything, for reasons you couldn't trace in an eternity of trying. But young as I was, it seemed to me that I did understand a little of what Aunt Sam was up to. Her friendship with my grandmother was close and warm, but she felt there was a flaw in it, a hairline fracture no one else would notice but which remained a tender spot between the two of them. Aunt Sam had determined to mend that fracture, to seal the friendship whole again, and she had decided that the act which signified completion would be for my grandmother to play music once more. It was a symbolic gesture, no more than that but no less too, and important to Aunt Sam.

I imagined that I began to understand a little. She was wealthy and famous, but Aunt Sam was lonesome too.

She missed having a family. This realization made me think of my family and though it didn't entirely reconcile me to the irksome fact, I began to feel somewhat mollified. And I thought that if it was in the cards that I had to have a family, I wanted Aunt Samantha Barefoot included.

One of the telephone calls had been from a radio station in Asheville. They wanted Aunt Sam to come to the studio for an interview, and she agreed to do it if she could bring a few friends. "Would you like to see a radio broadcast?" she asked.

"Yes," I said.

So then we were all in her big Cadillac, dressed in our Sunday best, riding to station WWNC. "Wonderful Western North Carolina," the announcers added, after giving the call letters, and of course my father always transformed the letters to different phrases: *Wildest Werewolves in North Carolina, Woolly Worm Night Crawlers*, and so forth.

At the station they gave us a short tour, showing us banks of exotic knobs and dials and switches, and a wall of photographs of famous people who had visited: Uncle Dave Macon, Little Jimmy Dickens, A. P. Carter, Woody Guthrie, and a platoon of others I'd never heard of. The proud young man showed us a blank space in the wall and said, "Here's where we'll put Miz Barefoot's picture." She was to be inserted between the Blue Sky Boys and Henry Wallace.

Then he led us into a room with two rows of folding chairs. We were to sit here and watch through the big soundproof window. Aunt Sam said that my grandmother was to be interviewed also and asked if they would need a voice check. My grandmother said that they wouldn't need a voice check, whatever in creation that was, because she didn't intend to talk on the radio.

There followed a long and predictable argument which Aunt Sam finally won. She told my grandmother that she was about to go on tour with a new group, the Briar Rose Ramblers, and they desired all the publicity they could get. She wanted her cousin to say a few words for the sake of local appeal; she didn't want people thinking she was some Brooklyn musician who had learned everything she knew from records. It was a matter of good business, she said, and that sentence was the clincher. My grandmother was proud of her business acumen. Didn't she always get the best prices going every Saturday for her ten pounds of butter and three dozen eggs?

It was quite exciting and I suffered only one punishing disappointment. The interviewer was an announcer named Reed Bascom, a short bald pudgy man with mushy hands. From his radio voice I'd pictured him as looking something like Johnny Weismuller, only more sophisticated. Worse than that, he patted me on the head.

We sat in the chairs and watched the interview through the window and heard it from a small loudspeaker overhead. It mostly went off very well. My grandmother marched to the microphone with the same tight-lipped grittiness she might evince for a leg amputation and when she was introduced to the radio audience, said, *Hello, folks* distinctly.

Almost all the questions were asked of Aunt Sam and my grandmother's main task was to stand by the microphone without passing out. When Aunt Sam explained that she was in these parts to visit her kinfolks, especially to visit her cousin Annie Barbara Sorrells, Mr. Bascom turned to her and asked a bland question or two. She answered succinctly and firmly.

Then he asked what sort of musical instrument she performed on and she replied, "Oh, I just play second fiddle to Cousin Sam."

That was her joke, the only one I ever heard her make. No one laughed or so much as chuckled, not even my father. We were stunned. I have an image of the three of us sitting in the little room with our mouths gaped open like coal scuttles, but surely this picture is a later emendation. We were actually too shocked to open our mouths.

"Now that's a promise, Annie B.," Aunt Sam crowed. "I'm going to hold you to that!"

Mr. Bascom appeared confused by this exchange and turned again to Aunt Sam to conclude the interview. It finished up pretty smooth except for one awkward moment when he said that some people claimed country music was getting too commercial, too far away from its old-time folk roots, and Aunt Sam replied that some people didn't know cow shit from cake batter.

The remaining remarks were hastily spoken and Mr. Bascom gave a signal to the engineer and the ON THE AIR sign went dark and they came into our little room. There was some busy leave-taking, Aunt Sam signed a publicity photo she had brought, and we went away.

Driving slowly home, Aunt Sam hummed a song. Her happiness shone in her like candlelight and she said once more, "I take your words as a promise, Annie Barbara, and I'm holding you to it."

My grandmother looked out at the green and yellow fields sliding beside us like a cool river and said nothing. We knew, three of us knew, that her first joke had been her last.

But if Aunt Sam considered it a promise, then so it was, and my grandmother would gnaw live rattlesnakes sooner than break a promise. The evening before she was to leave we all gathered in that sacrosanct corner of the house, the musty sun parlor. My grandmother hadn't touched a string instrument in nearly fifty years, but she agreed to accompany Aunt Sam on the piano. The piano was in disastrous condition since no one in our house played any more. The keys were chipped and broken, the strings green and rusty, and the notes that were not out of tune were mostly ciphers.

Nevertheless the bargain had been sealed, and my grandmother sat on the wobbly stool while Aunt Sam stood beside her with her fiddle and struck up "Come

All You Fair and Tender Ladies." It sounded very strange, and not entirely beautiful. They played two choruses and then Aunt Sam sang.

> *"Come all you fair and tender ladies,*
> *Take warning how you court young men,*
> *For they are like a bright star of a summer evening,*
> *They first appear and then they're gone."*

Her singing transfigured the music entirely. She had a dark contralto that sounded like it had mellowed in an oak barrel for slow decades, a voice as rich as damask soaked in burgundy wine. The song began to take on strength and shape. In the middle of a chorus Aunt Sam stopped singing and fiddling and all the music was my grandmother's harmony chords with so many notes missing. She played on, hesitant but unfaltering, and those wistful broken chords sounded like the harmony that must lie beneath all the music ever heard or thought of—tremulous, melancholy, constant. It was a music you might hear down in the autumn grass on a cold hillside. Then Aunt Sam joined in again and the song finished out with a lingering sweetness.

We were silent for a long space.

Then came the rottenest moment. My father said, "Well then, if that's the song you choose, I'm going to get Jess to sing. I want to hear 'The Green Laurel.' That's got a verse in it I'm partial to."

I fought against the suggestion like a wild dog, but it was no use. Nothing would do but for me to stand there in the middle of the floor and sing. I did it. Staring down at the scraped and battered toes of my shoes didn't help much, but it was less embarrassing than to look up and see Aunt Sam and my grandmother holding hands like schoolgirls and listening to me in seraphic rapture.

I made sure to include the verse my father wanted to hear:

> *"I have often wondered why women love men,*
> *But more times I've wondered how men can love*
> *them;*

They're men's ruination and sudden downfall,
And they cause men to labor behind the stone
wall."

My face burned like a comet; I mumbled and choked.
I couldn't sing then and I can't sing now. If I could sing—
sing, I mean, so that another human being could bear
to hear me—I wouldn't sit scribbling this story of long
ago time.

Helen

It seemed that there were four of us in a hunting cabin high on a mountain near the Tennessee border, Uncle Luden, Johnson Gibbs, my father, and me. And it seemed that it began to snow the second day we were there; in the late afternoon little bitter papery flakes came down in nervous spirals. It wasn't supposed to amount to much, but when we woke early the third morning there was well over a foot of the fluffy stuff, driven in scallops by a bluff wind. We decided to wait our deer hunting until the weather improved.

But it kept on snowing.

We amused ourselves with poker and setback and eating. The others drank a little whiskey, but I was too young. We didn't worry, but by that evening had started to feel a little cabin-bound. Our manners grew gentler; four of us in close quarters might prove a tedious business.

That night we stayed awake late, swapping lies and jokes about hunting, cars, sports. The others pulled a little more steadily at the whiskey, and a cozy lassitude suffused their talk and there were long passages of silence.

*I began to feel a little as a stranger among them. They
knew different things than I did. It seemed that they
were willing to tell me, but I didn't know what to ask.
If they had talked about women I would have had some
questions, but they never entered upon the subject. I
thought it curious that they hadn't; maybe they were
regarding my youth. No, that wouldn't be the reason.*

*After midnight the pauses lengthened and the comfy
drowsiness deepened, the fire sinking to orange-and-red
embers. They decided it was time for bed. I was still
wide awake, but did not demur. I kicked off my unlaced
boots and stripped off my shirt and heavy pants and
climbed into a top bunk. There I lay on my back with
my hands beneath my head, staring at the ceiling in
which I could barely make out the board edges and pine
knots. I heard the wind sifting the papery snow in the
oak trees and laurels.*

*They fell asleep one by one, their breathing steadied
and slowed and purred. Now and then one of them would
shift in his bunk like a log shifting in a campfire. I lay
thinking of many things, but nothing of winter. In my
mind was the light of summer and its grass smells and
sweat and dusty roads. I thought a little why we had
come here, what it would be like to kill a deer.*

*My thoughts were interrupted when Johnson Gibbs in
the lower bunk spoke in his sleep. I couldn't make out
the word the first time. He spoke again, thickly but
comprehensibly in the reddened dark: "Helen." Then he
said nothing more, but now there was true silence in the
cabin, no one turning or half-snoring, and I realized I
was holding my breath. I let it out carefully. And then
Uncle Luden asleep in the top bunk on my right spoke
the word: "Helen."*

*I could tell from his voice that he was asleep, and at
first I thought he was only repeating in dream the name
Johnson had uttered. But wouldn't it have changed in
his mind, undergone the usual alchemy? Maybe it was
someone they both knew, someone they happened to be*

*dreaming about at the same time. It was a farfetched
notion, but it amused me and I elaborated upon the
fancy for a while.*

*Then I heard my father in the other lower bunk roll
over and mutter a word. I couldn't hear it distinctly,
only a liquid-nasal murmur: " . . . llnn . . ." But now I
took it for granted that it was a transfiguration of the
familiar name* Helen.

*There was a woman I had never heard of before and
she was powerful in their three lives. No, that was not
possible. There was no secret like that for them to share.
They didn't share secrets anyhow.*

*The room waited; I couldn't hear them breathe now.
The fire had gone all down, only a pinkish gleam furred
over with gray ash. Suddenly—all at the same time—
each of the three stirred in his bed. I couldn't see them,
but recognized from the sound of the movement that
they now sat bolt upright in their bunks, their hands
flat on the mattresses. They were still not awake, but
each of them stared open-eyed and sightless into the
space of the room in front of the fireplace. As one man
they gasped, like divers coming out of the ocean. They
remained sitting, all three, breathing hoarsely, staring
and not seeing.*

*I couldn't see them. I couldn't see anything, but I
knew what they were doing. I too stared forward into
the room, straining to see. . . what? I knew I couldn't
look into their dreams, I had no desire to. But the ten-
sion caught me up, and I tried to sculpt from the darkness a shape I might recognize.*

*Little by little—yet all in a single instant—I saw
something. I thought that I saw. Framed by glossy black
hair, a face appeared there, the features blurred by a veil
and yet familiar to me, I fancied, if I could remember
something long ago and in a distant place. Then there
was no face. If something had actually appeared, it
lasted no longer than an after-image upon the retina.
But if I had seen something, then it was her,* Helen, *I
had glimpsed.*

Now the others lay back again. Their breathing slowed and quietened. Now they would dream no more of Helen; each would follow his own strange travels in the forests of dream; their sleepings would no longer touch.

I was disturbed most of all by the unplaceable familiarity of the vision. Who was this woman with thick black hair and those penetrating brown eyes? I thought and thought with no success and grew irritated and tired of myself. The room began to gray with predawn light reflecting from the snow and I fell asleep and dreamed of summer and a bright yellow field of oats.

I woke to the sound of sausage sizzling and water pouring. They were all up and about, and I scrambled down quickly and got dressed. In the kitchen, the only other room here, they went about their tasks, a little dull maybe from the evening whiskey. They gave me Good morning as I sat at the table and began to observe them closely.

No secret seemed to obtain among them. They were as open and careless as ever before. Even so, I felt myself at a distance from them, left out, and I felt too a small gray sense of shame, as if I'd gone through their pockets while they slept. But nothing passed among them that I could detect.

During breakfast my father informed me that we were leaving. Though the snow had stopped, they had decided the weather was no good for hunting and that we were returning home. I nodded dumbly.

They packed up and I packed hurriedly and went back to the cast-iron range to wash the tin plates and cups. They stripped the bunks and swept. When I finished washing up and had damped down the cookstove fire, I sat at the table while they loaded the gear. They waited in the car and still I sat there, gazing about the cabin.

In a few minutes I heard the sound of boots on the rough porch planking. The door opened and Johnson

183

Gibbs stood solidly in it. His blue eyes were very bright. There was full sunlight now and it made a burning glare on the snow. Against this harsh light Johnson's figure loomed black, black as velvet, blackly burning, and his voice sounded deep and hollow:

"Well, Jess, are you one of us or not?"